The Samu:

A Lega
Early Christians

Cathy Brueggemann Beil

Cereus Publications

"Neither do men light a candle, and put it under a bushel, but on a candlestick; and it giveth light unto all that are in the house.

The Samurai And The Tea

A Legacy of Japan's Early Christians

First Revised Edition 2003

ISBN 1-59109-380-5

Acknowledgements

The Japanese Martyrs were not in the original concept of this book. But once I learned their story, there was no question they would appear on these pages. I pray this work does honor to their sacrifice. My heartfelt thanks to the following: Tak Nomura, a Japanese American, who lived in the Internment Camps and loves America. Bill Clements, the artist who introduced me to the idea that Dr. Nagai and St. Maximilian Kolbe had met in Nagasaki, Japan. Father Paul Glynn, who graciously allowed me to use material from his book, A Song For Nagasaki. Yoshimi Ide, a Nagasaki Catholic, who answered so many questions. Michael Furukawa your web page, www.ajawarvets.com/ was an invaluable resource.

The Keiko Institute provided a wealth of information on the Hidden Christians. The Japan Information & Cultural Center and countless others are in my debt.

Dedication

I want to thank Aunt Juanita and Uncle John Domaschko, had it not been for your gentle inquiries, I might never have finished this book. You believed in my dreams and nudged me towards fulfilling them, thank you! Judy Vinegar, your interest spurred me on.

Jo Miller, you gave freely to this work and became so much more than a faceless editor. Through the Japanese Martyrs, we became friends. Gary Barnett, you were the young boy who always wanted to hear the story. Christopher and Maggie Barnett, I'll always be honored that you wanted to be the first to actually buy a copy of the book.

Mom, you waited for me to find time for you between writing and the rest of my life. Rick and Patti, I won't forget that so many years ago it was you who offered me a quiet place to write on a "real" computer. And Rick, your support, help and belief in my work are things I can never repay. Dan & Mary, with your children, your love and kindness are blessings in my life. Anna, you were tremendous with your help. Regina you read each word, thank you! Joe, you gave me the ideas of a soldier - you were ours, after all. Steven, Michael, Susan and dear Matthew, each of you are a part of the experience that led me to the writing life. Ed, thanks for all the technical assistance.

I offer this work with a prayer for our families, for Mom and for Dad, who is part of us too.

Last but not least to my sons, Wayne and Nicholas, and my husband, Wayne, I thank you from the very depths of my heart. How often you watched as I sailed off into flights of fancy. Though you didn't understand this constant need of mine, you accepted my crazy hunger for words and stories. How blessed I am to have each of you. May the saints of God surround you and lead you to Him not only in this life but also in the next.

CHAPTER ONE

There were two of them. Sleek, shiny swords with lacquered scabbards mounted on a wooden rack. Michael removed the longer one, admiring it in his grip. It was an ancient samurai sword. Inlaid dragons decorated each end of the handle. Each dragon faced the other, as if ready to leap into combat. The dragon nearest the blade bore the appropriate face of victory. The sword Michael held was a *katana*—meaning long sword. The *saya,* or scabbard, was a lacquered crimson with gold-plated bands circling the tip and the base. The crimson and gold wrappings may not have been the originals to this ancient object, but they could have been, Michael thought. He could picture the Samurai who once held this sword of honor.

The swords made him proud of his Japanese ancestry. He had heard that the samurai were brave men of *bushido*, meaning they followed the way of the warrior. *Bushido* demands, above all else, the willingness to face death. And facing death willingly means conquering fear.

Michael's attachment to the swords wasn't only because they belonged to an ancient Samurai ancestor, but because they made Michael feel as if he had bushido. He tightened his grip around the handle of the sword. He imagined an enemy before him. He spread his feet into a *kata* stance and thrust the sword forward.

"Be careful with those, Michael," said his father, who had entered the room silently.

"I am being careful, Dad! I was just looking at it. No one else was in the room. I wasn't aiming it at any one!"

Leave it to his father to make him feel like a kid. He was constantly worried that Michael was going to mess up. It seemed all he ever said were things like, don't touch, be careful, or watch out. He was fourteen years old and his father treated him like a child.

"Michael, not only are certain precautions necessary to prevent injury to you or anyone else, but under no circumstances is the blade ever to be touched with bare hands or fingers. The acidic natural oils can cause rusting of the blade. These swords are valuable artifacts and should be treated as such." His father took the katana from him and made sure the blade was in the special cloth as he thrust it back into the scabbard.

"But Dad...I didn't touch the blade. I was just getting it down to pack. Grandmother told me to start in here." In defiance, Michael reached out and seized the *tanto*, the second shorter sword, less than twelve inches in cutting length. He tried not to look in the direction of his father as he wrapped it in the soft red cloth. Only after he had placed it carefully in the wooden storage box did he glance at him. Then he quickly looked away and left the room. How could he travel the way of the warrior when he wasn't even allowed to hold a sword?

Michael was sure he would never have *bushido*. His father wouldn't let him. He was only four years old when his mother died; she wasn't even a memory that he could call his own. He knew her only through the photograph that sat on the piano and the stories Grandmother sometimes told.

His father's parents, the Brogans, were German immigrants. But no one called his dad a German-American. Descendents of European immigrants were

6

simply known as Americans. Descendents of Japanese immigrants, like Michael, bore the label Japanese-Americans. It wasn't as if a label were necessary. All you had to do was look at their faces. The almond-shaped eyes, the dark straight hair and the tint of their skin set them apart.

His father didn't know how it was to look like you didn't even belong in your own family. He remembered the time he overheard his third-grade teacher say to his dad, "I think it is so wonderful that you adopted Michael."

"Michael is not adopted," his father had said. "He is my biological son."

Michael's face had burned in anger. Stupid woman. He had had to bite his lip so that he wouldn't cry. If his father had not been with him, he knew he would have. Instead he remained silent, not even talking once they were in the car.

"Don't pay attention to things like that, Michael," his father had said on the way home. But Michael had paid attention. How could he not? He looked nothing like his father and his mother was gone.

"Come on, Michael," his father had coaxed. "Don't sit there and sulk. You should know that what you look like doesn't determine who you are. Besides, I certainly didn't resemble my dad."

"Maybe not, but I bet your teachers didn't think you were adopted."

"No, but I used to wish I had been." His father had laughed his thunderous laugh as if the joke were supposed to make him feel better about not looking like an American.

Not only will we never look alike, we'll never understand one another, thought Michael as he went in search of his grandmother.

He found her in the kitchen making lunch. "The swords are packed, Grandmother."

She looked up from the black lacquer trays she was preparing and smiled at him. "Are you hungry, Michael?"

7

"Not very," he answered. He didn't tell her that his father had ruined his appetite.

"Don't fix anything for me," his father said as he followed him into the kitchen. "I have to attend a faculty meeting tonight and I need to get home and finish the report I was working on." He patted Michael on the back then walked out the door saying, "Help your grandmother now."

"I will," Michael said. After the door shut behind his father Michael looked at his grandmother and said, "I wish you didn't have to leave. I don't know if I can take Dad when you're not around."

"Why do you say that Michael? Your father's feelings for you are no different than mine. He only wants what is best for you."

"You don't understand, Grandmother. He treats me like a little kid."

"I understand more than you realize, Michael. Your father is a good man. Now, go sweep the porch steps for me, will you? Lunch is nearly ready."

Later they sat in the garden and ate the Japanese foods she had fixed. Michael could hear the baby green frogs splashing in the pond. The leaves leaned gently toward the ground in the afternoon breeze. He tried not to think about the fact that he wouldn't be able to come here anymore. After his grandmother moved, someone else would sit in her wonderful garden. The little pond and the perfectly arranged stones had always given Michael a sense of peace when his world was in chaos.

The patio furniture had already been moved so Michael and his grandmother sat on the concrete steps near the porch.

"I'm going to miss this place," she said, filling his glass with tea and offering him a *daifuku* - a sweet snack that looked like a large, flat marshmallow.

His grandmother was moving to Lexington, KY. She had been offered a position with the Japan-American Society of Kentucky and would be teaching at the University. It was nearly a two-hour drive and Michael could already taste the pain of her absence.

8

His sadness became a lump that grew heavy in his throat. He tried to force it away by taking a bite of the soft snack. It was better than he'd expected. Many of the recipes she wanted him to try were as alien to him as his mother and the past he shared with her. His grandmother watched as he finished the last bite.

"My *obaason*, grandmother, would make these whenever she could. We loved them as children. I am glad I finally made them myself. It's the red bean paste that keeps them moist."

"Great," thought Michael, just what I didn't need to know. But then again it was good that she had waited until he had finished to tell him what was in it, otherwise he may not have been able to eat it.

"Nearly everything is packed," she said. "You were a great help, Michael."

"I was very careful with the swords, Grandmother," he told her.

"Those swords have been in our family for generations. Someday they will belong to you." Michael hoped that she was giving him a hint about his birthday gift next week. He had overheard her discussing his present with his father just the other day. He didn't hear what the gift was, but did hear his grandmother say, "It is just one of the items I am going to slowly pass on to him, Richard. I hope you don't mind." Michael couldn't wait.

He didn't let on to her that he suspected in any way the gift that was to come. He finished his tea and helped as she cleared the dishes. As he followed her into the kitchen Michael realized how young she looked for a grandmother. She was a small woman, her hair cut fashionably short. How could someone so delicate be the strongest person he knew?

"I'm going to miss you, Grandmother," Michael told her.

"And I will miss you, my *magomusuko,* grandson, but you will be fine. Your father needs you very much."

"I'm more like you than him, and it's going to be awful not having you close by."

9

"Perhaps it will be for the best. You need to find the link that binds you to your father, Michael. I'm afraid I've stood between the two of you."

"But that's just it. There isn't a link. I'm Japanese-American. He's not."

"Michael, I was going to wait until your birthday to give you something, but I think the time is now." She locked the dishwasher door into place, took the dishrag from Michael and folded it on the sink.

Michael tried to control his excitement. He just knew she was going to give him the swords now. They were neatly packed in the box. He may not even have to say anything to his father. He could just slide them beneath his bed at home; and like his grandmother, wait until the time was right to tell him.

But when she came back into the kitchen, the box she was carrying was all wrong. He had never seen this box before. He certainly had not come across it while packing. The swords he'd wrapped so carefully were in a long, narrow, wooden box. The one she placed on the counter before him was just a bit taller than the box his roller blades came in last Christmas. He stared at the unknown gift. It was made of smooth wood, with an elaborate handle on the top. Michael struggled to hide his disappointment, "What is this?" He certainly didn't have to pretend surprise.

"Open it," she instructed him.

The handle at the top was not for opening the box but for carrying it. There was a door on the front of the box with a small latch. Michael opened it. Knowing it wasn't the gift he wished for still didn't prepare him for the contents. Two shelves inside the box held the treasures his grandmother was passing on to him.

"A tea set?" his voice squeaked betraying his dismay.

"It's not a regular tea set. It is a very special family heirloom. The utensils inside are for the Japanese Tea Ceremony, the *Chado*, or Way of the

Tea." She looked so proud of her gift. Michael struggled to hide his disappointment.

"Thanks Grandmother. Thanks a lot."

"Take the pieces out, Michael. Feel them in your hands."

Michael reached into the box and removed a bowl. Not a cup, mind you, but a bowl. It had no handle as Michael expected.

"In *Chado,* a bowl called a *chawan* is used," his grandmother told him. "The *chawan* is cupped in the palm of one's hands rather than held aloft by a handle." She gently took the *chawan* from Michael then opened his hand and placed it again on his palm. Heavy glaze gave it a dark amber color. The bowl gently sloped from a tiny grooved base, opening to a deep center well. The rim was painted with small white crosses.

Michael thought of the elegant swords and then looked at the tea set and wondered what in the world ever possessed his grandmother to give him this instead of the swords. Did she want to make a sissy of him or what? How could she humiliate him like that?

He wasn't rude enough to ask her that question but she must have known he was thinking it. Because as soon as he looked at her she said, "In simplicity lies great beauty."

Did she think that made him feel better? It only made him feel worse. He had so wanted the swords. He didn't care about simplicity, or beauty. He cared about *bushido* and the way of the warrior. He felt hot tears of disappointment and swallowed hard to stop them.

"And that's not all, Michael. I have arranged for you and me to attend classes for the Tea Ceremony. Our first lesson is tomorrow evening." It was then Michael realized there was something worse than the gift itself. Classes? Classes to learn about tea parties? He felt sick.

He refused his grandmother's offer of a ride and walked home, carrying his tea set and trying to get over his disappointment. He had looked forward to

11

summer, especially summer with the swords. He had even visualized showing off the swords to some of the guys at school, maybe taking classes on fencing or some other samurai type activity. Those kinds of things would make the other guys treat him like one of them. Now he could only hope they would never learn about the tea set or the classes. He had enough trouble fitting in.

The next evening found him sitting in a plain room in downtown Cincinnati, waiting with his grandmother for a teacher to tell them about tea. The door behind them opened and a middle-aged woman came into the room. She wore a soft blue kimono with snowflakes falling around the hem.

She gave a deep ceremonial bow that Michael and his grandmother tried to match. "I am Mrs. Osaka. I am very pleased to meet you and share the history of tea."

When his grandmother just nodded, Michael did the same. At least they didn't expect him to be jolly and do a lot of talking.

Mrs. Osaka waved her hand over the table to indicate the utensils and said, "While many people believe that *Chanoyu,* or Tea Ceremony is for women and *geishas*, it was originally performed only by men; trained practitioners. The *chajin* were tea men and only later was the custom passed on to women.

"Many of the *chajin* were of the samurai class. As warriors they were drawn to *Chado* as a way to ease their cares and calm their fears."

Oh brother, thought Michael. He didn't believe that the samurai had been afraid - and he certainly didn't believe that tea parties calm the fears of such brave men.

Mrs. Osaka picked up a tea bowl and said, "Each movement in *Chado* is part of the art of the ceremony. Remember, every single encounter in life is unique and can never be repeated, *ichigo ichie*. Therefore each encounter has special meaning and the host prepares each tea with deep sincerity. The movements are important."

12

With her right hand she raised the tea bowl and said, "Always pick up with your right hand and place in the palm of your left hand. Then turn the bowl clockwise three times as it rests in your palm."

What a bunch of baloney, thought Michael. Like it really mattered how you held a cup of tea or whether you rotated it clockwise in your hand. Darn it all, why did Grandmother do this to him? He thought again of the elegant swords, he'd been so sure that possessing them would gain him at least a form of grudging respect.

"Please study and practice each movement for the next class," Mrs. Osaka was saying. Michael glanced at his grandmother. He wondered how long this would go on. It felt like the class would never end. Really! How much instruction did he need to put a bowl in his hands and rotate it?

Mrs. Osaka was still droning on, "Ancient tradition tells of a young monk who could not remain awake during meditations. He became so frustrated that he tore off his eyelids and threw them on the ground." Mrs. Osaka's own eyes grew large as she told the rest of the story. "What do you think? Right on that very spot a plant grew. Another monk brewed the leaves of that plant for his hungry brothers and they were all re-energized after drinking the concoction! The plant was called *cha,* or tea and no longer did young monks have trouble keeping their eyes open." She smiled at Michael and said, "I don't know how true the story is, but oddly enough the soaked leaves do look a lot like an eyelid."

The next day Michael's grandmother called to cancel the next tea class. He was relieved until he learned the reason. "I am leaving in two days Michael," she said. "The family buying my house would like to move in early. There was no reason for me to refuse since my job starts next week anyway and the extra few days will give me time to get used to Lexington."

Michael tightened his grip on the cordless phone, but didn't answer her. He couldn't; there was a huge lump in his throat.

"Michael, I'm sorry," she said. "Please try to be happy for me. Though I'll miss you and your father, I'm also excited about this opportunity."

Michael still did not speak. He did not tell her that it was okay.

"I'll stop by tomorrow to say good-bye," she said. Michael heard the receiver click as she hung up on his sorrow. He wanted her to be happy. But he wanted her to be happy two blocks away; where he could find her when he needed her. Why even the tea set would be bearable, maybe even funny if Grandmother was nearby. She had always been there for Michael when he needed her.

And then Michael realized - it was time he was there for her. She deserved his support for a change. He decided to do something nice for her, to show her that he was happy if she was. He went down to the family room and got everything ready. He hoped she would know without his saying it, that he was ready to say good-bye like a man.

The next day Michael couldn't wait for his grandmother to arrive. When the doorbell rang he went to answer it. For the first time in his life, he was sorry he'd always refused to wear the kimonos she'd bought him. Years ago she quit trying and now he had none that would fit him. He tried to make the best of it and bowed low like Mrs. Osaka.

"Come," he told her, leading her into the family room. "Michael, what is all this?" she asked, looking in wonder at the low table and the makings of tea. The crinkles around her mouth threatened to turn into a smile. He knew she was happy.

"Well it isn't perfect, especially since we had only one class, but I wanted to see you off with a tea ceremony. It is my way of saying thank you for being there for me all these years."

She brushed a tear from her eye and said, "Michael, you are such a dear!"

He waved his hand over the table as Mrs. Osaka had done and bowed low once more, waiting for his grandmother to be seated first. Michael then folded his legs beneath him and sat opposite her. He had gone to great pains to duplicate what he could remember of the tea ceremony movements.

He poured hot water from the teapot over the powdered tea and with the bamboo whisk, whipped it to a frothy green. He passed the *chawan* to his grandmother. She held it in her palm and turned it three times, and sipped from the *chawan*. Then it was Michael's turn.

He picked it up with his right hand and placed it in the palm of his left. Concentrating on his movements, he turned the *chawan* clockwise three times. He bowed to his grandmother and brought the *chawan* to his lips, swallowing the bitter, grassy tasting liquid. As the warmth spread to his stomach, his legs began to tingle. He was not used to sitting like this.

A soft chime tingled in the distance and a breeze passed over his face causing him to blink. When he opened his eyes he thought he was dreaming. He was no longer in his house with his grandmother. He was sitting in a garden and the garden was full of people!

CHAPTER TWO

Michael was sitting in the same position he had been in with his grandmother. But the place where she had sat was vacant. His belly was still warm with tea, and yet he was far from the room in which he had sipped it.

The people around him were strangers - and there was something strange about them. The boys, who wore jeans, had them turned up about two inches at the cuff. Their hair was slicked back and the women wore dresses that looked like the ones his grandmother wore in old photos. The garden too, was different. Michael was certain he had never been there before. A radio was playing softly in the background. It sounded like the oldies station his dad sometimes listened to.

"Are you here to help?" The voice belonged to a boy who looked to be a few years older than Michael. His face was that of a Japanese-American.

"Where am I?" Michael asked. "Who are you?"

"I happen to live here. I think that makes you the one who should answer the questions. What are you doing here?"

"I don't know. I must be dreaming," said Michael. He was so confused and afraid. Whatever had happened, Michael knew it was bizarre. Where had his grandmother gone and how did he get here?

"Well you're dreaming in my back yard. So if you don't mind, get out of here. We need workers not daydreamers."

"Please, help me," Michael must have sounded dreadful because the boy's anger seemed to fade.

"Look, I don't know what your problem is, or what kind of help you need. But we still have to clear out our entire house. Your family may have taken care of their belongings, but we haven't made a dent in ours."

"Daniel, come help me with the kitchen bundle," a woman's voice called.

"Look, I have to help my mother. If you're going to stick around, how about helping out?"

Michael certainly had no other options. How could he get back home if he didn't even know where he was? He couldn't just sit in this guy's backyard. "What do you want me to do?"

"Tell me your name for starters," said the boy. "Mine is Daniel Endo."

"Okay, I'm Michael Brogan," Michael said, reaching out to shake Daniel's hand.

Daniel grasped Michael's hand and shook it firmly, "Brogan? How did you manage a name like that? You don't look like a Brogan."

"My mother was Japanese-American, my father is not."

"Wow," Daniel seemed impressed. I thought that was illegal. Anyway, we better hustle. Mother doesn't like to be kept waiting."

"Who are all these people?" Michael asked as he followed Daniel into the house.

"These people are all friends of ours. They don't like what the government is doing. They want to help. But the only thing they can really do is help pack us off like the government wants anyway."

"What is the government doing?"

Daniel looked hard at Michael and said, "You're way out in left field aren't you? They're sending us away, that's what."

As they made their way into the house Michael saw people packing books into boxes. Others were

17

carrying furniture out into the front yard. Through the open door he saw cars parked on the street. People were getting out of the cars and milling about the yard looking at the furniture. Then Michael realized something.

The cars were all old models. There wasn't a modern car on the street. As a matter of fact, he had never seen such old cars. But they weren't "old" - old cars. They were new, old cars. An icy finger of fear tickled the back of his neck. He thought he knew the answer to the question, but he asked it anyway.

"Daniel, what is the date?"

Daniel stopped in his tracks and turned to look at Michael. "Are you touched in the head or something?"

"Just tell me what day it is."

"It's May 20th," Daniel said as they entered the kitchen.

Apparently, Daniel's mother didn't know much about packing. She had placed a large sheet on the kitchen floor and on top of the sheet she had thrown all sorts of things from the cabinets. There were a couple of pots and pans, silverware, an iron, containers with lids and several tin plates used for camping. She was bending over an old teakettle, rolling it in a bath towel. She placed the bundle in the middle of the mess she had collected on the sheet. She grabbed a pile of clothing off the counter and placed that in the bundle too.

"Now, you grab that end, Daniel," she said as she picked up an edge of the sheet. Mrs. Endo took the corner from Daniel and tied it into a tight knot. Then she looked at Michael and said, "And who are you?"

"My name is Michael Brogan."

"Hello Michael, it's nice to meet you. Now could you hand me that corner by your foot?"

Michael did as he was told. Mrs. Endo then took the remaining two corners and tied a knot over the previous one.

"Please take this bundle into the parlor,

18

Daniel." Daniel hoisted the bundle over his shoulder and headed toward the front room.

"I could show you a better way to pack that stuff," Michael said, following him. "I just helped my grandmother pack. There's a neater way to do things you know."

Daniel dropped the bundle near another one that was a lot bigger. "Oh, so you're an expert?"

"No, but why not use boxes like those people in the other room?"

"How many boxes can your grandmother carry? Because if you packed your grandmother's things in boxes, she won't be taking much to the camp."

"The camp?" Michael asked.

"What's wrong with you? Did you get hit on the head or something? Didn't they tell you? You're only allowed to take what you can carry? I can carry a heck of a lot more in this sheet than you can in a box."

Michael was confused again. "Before, when you told me it was May 20th, you didn't say what year it was."

"I'm starting to wonder if we need your help after all. You act like you just fell from the sky."

"Just tell me what year this is," Michael insisted.

"Sure, it's 1942. May 20th, 1942. Now what year were you expecting?"

That means Pearl Harbor was bombed by Japan only a few months ago, Michael thought. Aloud he said, "This can't be happening."

"Tell me about it," agreed Daniel. "We actually had FBI officers searching our house in the middle of the night. When they couldn't find anything incriminating they decided to take my father instead. They wouldn't tell us what they were looking for or what my father was being charged with. That was weeks ago and we still haven't heard from him. Now we are being forced from our homes. They are sending us to what they call 'relocation centers.' We don't want to relocate. But what we want doesn't count. Japanese-American means, American with no rights." Daniel's voice choked and he quickly wiped something from his eye.

"Daniel, I'm not supposed to be here," Michael said.

"Well go home then."

"That isn't what I mean. I'm not talking about this place. I am talking about this time. I am not from this time! I am from the future."

"You've snapped, huh?" Daniel looked at him sadly. "I hear it is happening to many of us, although usually it is the older ones. They just can't face what America has done to them. They believed in this country, that is why they came here in the first place. It isn't our fault Japan bombed Pearl Harbor. We aren't Japanese, we're Americans. But our face has made us the enemy."

Michael wished he would wake up. He wished if he couldn't wake up, that he could at least make the people in this dream understand he didn't belong there. Daniel clapped his hand on Michael's shoulder and said, "I'm not trying to run you off, but it's almost time for the curfew, you better get home, or the FBI will be snatching you, too."

Michael gulped and nearly choked on the wad of fear in his throat. "Daniel, I can't go home. I have no home in 1942. I am from 2002."

"You don't say! Well, here's an idea. Why not take us all to your home in 2002? Is everybody there as crazy as you?" Michael could see that Daniel thought he was crazy. And that wasn't going to help Michael. He had to figure this out, but in the meantime, he needed a place to stay.

"Can I just stay here with you? I won't be on the street after curfew if I'm here with you."

"And what about your grandmother and all those neat little boxes you have packed. Doesn't she need you?"

"I lied," Michael said. "I don't have a grandmother. I don't have anybody. I don't want to be alone if the FBI comes for me."

"What happened to your family?" Daniel wanted to know.

"My mother died when I was little. My dad is gone...I don't know where. And my grandmother is dead." Michael whispered a prayer asking forgiveness for the lie. He didn't want to kill off his grandmother or make his father disappear. But he had no choice.

"I don't know. You seemed okay at first, but you are definitely weird and I don't know if I can trust you. I'm the man of the house now that my father is gone, and I can't just let a stranger come and stay with us."

Michael tried to think of something he could do to prove to Daniel that he was trustworthy. But he knew there was nothing. Just when he thought he was about to be thrown in the street to be devoured by the FBI dogs, Daniel relented.

"Wait here. I'll be right back." And he turned and ran back into the house. When he came back moments later he said, "You can stay here for now. But if we find out you have lied to us, you will not only be thrown out; we'll give you to the FBI ourselves."

"Agreed," said Michael and hoped that the lies he'd already told could not be proven since he really didn't exist in this time yet anyway.

Michael noticed that most of the people had left and the old cars were gone from the street. It seemed they had taken everything with them. The front yard was empty of all the Endo's furniture.

Inside Mrs. Endo was sitting on the floor arranging dishes steaming with rice. "You've already met my mother," Daniel said. He pointed to a little girl about six years old and said, "Michael, this is my sister, Beth."

The little girl looked at him and said, "You sit by me." And so Michael did.

Mrs. Endo passed him a bowl of rice and Beth handed him two chopsticks. "Momma packed away our silverware. So we must eat with chopsticks. I can eat with chopsticks, but my dolly is having a hard time." She clutched a doll in her lap and Michael saw from the rice sticking to the doll's cheeks, that she was,

21

indeed, having a difficult time eating with the chopsticks.

Michael breathed a sigh of relief and silently thanked his grandmother for teaching him how to handle the little wooden sticks. Mrs. Endo led them in a prayer before the meal and then they picked up the chopsticks and began to eat.

"How have you been managing on your own, Michael?" asked Mrs. Endo.

Michael nearly panicked, trying to think of an answer when Daniel's mother provided it for him. "Have you been working on the farms around here?"

"Uh, yes…I've worked on farms," at least it wasn't a lie. He'd gone with his father a couple of times to pick apples at an orchard in the country.

"Which ones have you worked on?" she asked pouring him a glass of milk. "I know most of the farmers around here."

But he needn't have worried about finding an answer. He stuck his chopsticks into his rice bowl in order to reach for his glass of milk and they stood, like two shovels thrust in the earth. Mrs. Endo gave a small gasp of alarm and Daniel immediately grabbed the chopsticks out of the rice and placed them lengthwise across the rim of the bowl. He whispered to Michael, "You idiot!"

Abruptly, Mrs. Endo stood up and said, "Excuse me, please." She almost ran from the room.

"What did I do wrong?" Michael asked.

"If I didn't know any better, I'd start believing you ARE from another time," Daniel muttered. "You haven't a clue how to act."

"I don't understand. What did I do?"

"There are certain things you never do with chopsticks. And one of those things you just did."

"But why? What difference does it make?"

"It is a custom during a funeral to place incense sticks into a special bowl to honor the dead, in the same way you just placed your chopsticks. It's a bad omen."

"Please, Daniel, go after her and tell her I am sorry."

22

"She'll be okay. She isn't really superstitious, but at a time like this, it's hard to shake the old ways. Besides, I told her you're touched in the head." Sure enough, Mrs. Endo returned a few moments later and they resumed their meal.

When they were finished, Mrs. Endo and Beth went into the kitchen to wash the dishes. She told the boys to unroll blankets on the floor for them to sleep on since not a stick of furniture was left in the house. Even the beds had been sold.

Michael was spreading out a soft quilt when he noticed a pile of belongings that had not been sold or packed away. There, in the corner of the room, was the cabinet his grandmother had given him.

Michael walked over and knelt down in front of it. He was sure it was the same cabinet. It had the same handle as his, the same smooth wood. He was about to open the door when he had an idea.

"Daniel, come here," he whispered.

Daniel came over and knelt beside him. "What?"

"I'm familiar with this cabinet. I know you think I am crazy, but this is the same cabinet my grandmother gave to me in my own time."

"Not that again! Look…"

"No, wait. Before you start telling me how crazy I am, let me prove to you that I am from the future."

"And how do you propose to do that?"

"Ask me a question. A question I wouldn't be able to answer if I had not seen inside this cabinet before."

"You're not off to a very good start if you want to impress me," Daniel said. "Because if you knew anything, you would know that it isn't a cabinet, it is a *chabako.*" But Daniel took pity on him once again saying, "You want to show me your powers? Okay, I'm game. Tell me what's inside the *chabako.*"

"Utensils. It holds utensils for Chado."

"Describe them in detail," Daniel commanded.

"The *chawan* is a dark amber color and it is decorated with tiny crosses around the rim."

Daniel reached across and opened the little door. "Well, how about that? You're right. Problem is, you could have seen inside this somehow when I wasn't looking." Michael gave up. He wasn't going to be able to convince Daniel that easily.

"Hey, I'm a fair kind of guy, so I'll give you another shot at it. Can you tell me what is on the bottom of the tea set?"

Michael wished he could go back to his own time and examine the pieces. But he'd been so disappointed with the gift; he had not even looked at them thoroughly. "I don't know," he told Daniel. "I never really looked at the bottom." I should have paid more attention, he thought. Tears were welling up behind his eyes. He tried to ignore them by asking Daniel, "So what does *chabako* mean?"

"It isn't so hard to figure out. It simply means, tea box. But don't look so down, buddy. I'm not going to throw you out just because you don't know all about this tea set." He then placed the *chawan* back on the shelf.

"Could I look at it now?" Michael asked.

"Help yourself."

Michael picked up the *chawan* and turned it over. He saw that he couldn't have read the inscription anyway, since it was written in Japanese.

Just then Mrs. Endo came back into the room. Beth followed; her doll in tow. "Goodnight Daniel," said Mrs. Endo. "You and Michael try to get some rest. Beth and I are going to go through the rest of the rooms and make sure we haven't forgotten anything.

"And Daniel, I wanted you to know, the tractor and plow sold for $25.00. The farmer who bought it took Bessie too," she said.

"But Mother!" Daniel objected.

"I know son, but we must sell it. Our time is running out. Otherwise we loose the equipment and the money."

"I'd rather have it destroyed. It is like standing by and watching everything you worked for being stolen."

"*Shikata ga nai,* it cannot be helped. We must take the compensation we are offered, Daniel. We cannot afford to loose everything because of pride. I'm certain we will be glad for every dollar one day."

"And the Americans are counting on that. That's why they offer us insults and expect us to be grateful for being cheated."

Mrs. Endo gave Daniel a sharp look and nodded in Beth's direction. "Let us not forget that we too, are Americans."

"I also can't forget the kindly American who offered to trade us our brand new Maytag washing machine for the old washboard under his arm," Daniel told her. "I'm sorry, Mother, but I can't forget the way he laughed at us after making his stupid offer."

But Michael wasn't listening anymore. Mrs. Endo's strange words, *Shikata ga nai,* had stirred the dust of memory in Michael's mind. His grandmother had said those very words once when she was telling Michael about something in her childhood.

"Have I ever told you about the evacuation?" his grandmother had asked him one day. Michael could not remember what he had answered. But he did remember what his grandmother had said.

"It was the spring of 1942. The Wartime Civil Control Administration ordered all Japanese-Americans in the valley to 'close our affairs promptly' and make arrangements for disposal of our personal property. We were given only a week to either sell our homes and possessions or find someone to care for them during our absence. We had no idea how long we would be gone or if we would ever come back. My mother was so proud of her brand new Maytag, and a disgusting man came by and offered her an old washboard in trade. He laughed as he said it and enjoyed my mother's worry over all that was happening. It broke my heart when we had to let our old cow, Bessie go. All of our furniture was sold for next to nothing and the people who bought it acted as though they had done us a great favor in giving us a few dollars.

25

"We were told to report for registration and to pack only what we could carry in two hands. Look around you, Michael. Can you imagine such a thing today?"

Michael could not imagine the scene his grandmother was painting. How could you decide from a lifetime of possessions what to take in just two hands?

"Mother gathered the things she knew we would need. She threw some pots and pans in a sheet and handed them to my brother, Daniel. Only the clothes that could be packed in two suitcases were taken to clothe the four of us. The rest had to be left behind. Our radios, cameras, and binoculars had already been confiscated by the authorities. They claimed it was contraband. And the FBI took my father away in the middle of the night."

And then she had said those words. The words Mrs. Endo had just spoken.

"*Shikata ga nai*, it cannot be helped. That was the old saying so many whispered in the camp. But we can learn from our past. I am proud to be an American. I am glad that you and I were born here; but in order to really understand who we are, it is essential to know from where we came.

"We arrived at the train station, with the tags bearing our family number, 12747, fastened to the buttons of our jackets. We struggled with the weight of the two sacks we each carried. The station was filled with hundreds of other families just like us. It was a huge moving day to say the least. But not one of us knew where they were taking us. It was horrible. We were forced from our homes, accused of being spies against our country, and shipped to places about which we knew nothing. I was lucky to have been a child at that time. It was so much harder for the teens and adults who understood what was going on. They knew that we were being rounded up like cattle; and that while most of us were American citizens, our rights were being taken away. We had not been convicted of any crimes and yet when we arrived at our destination we saw to our horror that we were indeed moving to prison camps.

"Barbed wire fences surrounded the camp and huge watchtowers hovered above us. We could see the guards standing in the tower, guns ready to stop us should we try to escape. I didn't understand all the implications. Yet, somehow I knew that a dark wound had pierced my childhood, bleeding my innocence, scabbing a portion of my life.

"Or maybe I simply sensed the darkness through Daniel. He was 17 years old and he knew more of what was happening. He had always been so playful before the camp, but after we were moved there, it was as if he went away, into a place inside himself that none could reach."

Of course! Michael nearly gasped at his realization.

His grandmother's brother was named Daniel. Her father's tractor and plow sold for $25.00 and she had a cow named Bessie. Michael was amazed it had taken him this long to figure it out. He didn't catch on right away because his grandmother's last name was Miki. But of course, that was her married name. His dad always called her Elizabeth, but as a child she must have been called, Beth. One piece of the puzzle clicked firmly in place. These strangers were his family!

Michael closed his eyes and rubbed his finger over the slightly raised letters on the bottom of the *chawan*. He wondered how long ago the brush strokes had been made.

His legs had grown stiff from kneeling and just as he started to shift them, they began to tingle.

CHAPTER THREE

Michael opened his eyes. He was standing less than three feet from a coffin that held the body of a man he did not know. People around him were crying. The building they were in appeared to be nothing more than a vacant barn, with a coffin situated in the center of the large structure. He scanned the crowd until he caught sight of a familiar face. Daniel stood next to the coffin. He was not crying, but Michael could tell he had been.

His mother stood with her arm around his shoulders and Beth clung to the hem of her dress. The man must be someone close to them, thought Michael.

He studied the man in the casket. Though older, he bore a striking resemblance to Michael. For the first time in his life, Michael realized he blended in with a large group of people. He looked into the faces of the strangers. Shiny black-haired heads, almond-shaped eyes, and dark-skinned bodies filled the barn. These were his ancestors. He carried a small imprint of each of these strangers within himself. Suddenly, Michael felt drawn to his past. He wanted to know more about these people and the man in the casket.

He was a bit surprised by the blood red rosary beads that entwined the man's fingers. While Michael was a Catholic himself, he had always pictured his ancestors as Buddhist or something.

Suddenly, Daniel walked up beside him. He grabbed Michael by the arm and led him from the barn.

As he met the cool night air, Michael was glad to escape the strangers in the barn and follow the only person here with whom he felt familiar.

"What's happening?" he asked.

"I don't understand why you ask these questions. You must already know. No one in camp is unaware that Grandfather was shot and killed by the guards," Daniel's voice answered in the darkness.

"Your grandfather?" He felt a sharp pang at the realization that this was his great-great-grandfather. He longed to tell Daniel who he was but could not. Instead he simply asked, "Why did they kill him? What did he do?"

"What did he do?" Daniel repeated Michael's question. His voice was hollow and each word was a pebble cast to the bottom of the abyss. "Oh, he committed a terrible crime! He had the nerve to gather rocks! He wanted to make a garden path for my grandmother. He saw a flat, pretty rock near the camp's outer fence. He told me that morning after breakfast that he was going to get it. It was broad daylight. Yet they shot and killed him because he broke a camp rule. We are fenced in here with guards for God's sake! What harm can be done by approaching the fence in daylight? He was an unarmed man, going after a rock and they gunned him down, shot him in the back." Daniel sliced away the tears that slid down his cheek. He straightened his shoulders and asked, "How long have you been hanging around here?"

Daniel's jaw tightened and his next words were a bad taste he spit in Michael's face, "And thanks for running out on us back home. Is that how you thank a friend? You just disappeared and we haven't heard from you till now."

"I disappeared all right! But I had no choice in the matter. I told you I am from the future. I haven't figured out a way to aim at my destinations. And I don't seem to have any control over when I leave a place." Michael answered.

"Of course, how could I forget? You just drop in from time to time. I wish we all had your power."

"Okay," Michael said. "I know you don't believe me. But somehow I am going to find a way to prove it to you."

Daniel stopped in front of a small outbuilding. It appeared to be an abandoned shack. But Michael noticed the sections where transformations had been made. Where there had once obviously been a door, scrap lumber had been nailed over the top of the doorway. This left a small opening at the bottom. A small door covered the opening and Daniel knelt to open it. He then crawled through to the other side. Michael stood in wonder at the small door. Daniel hissed in the darkness, "Well come on!"

Michael crawled in after him. "What is this place?" he asked looking around the room. It was surprisingly clean and empty. There was no furniture. An opening had been cut in the floor and a charcoal brazier stood in the hole. There, next to the hole was the tea box. Michael stared at it.

"What's the matter?" asked Daniel. "Still trying to figure out how to tell me some unknown secret about the *chabako*?"

"No," Michael answered and realized that it was useless to try to prove that he was from the future.

"Too bad. That ruins my fun," said Daniel.

"Well, that's a real shame, since my greatest ambition is to furnish you with fun."

"Why don't we call a truce? I'll admit I was pretty mad when you ran off like you did. I mean, after I talked my mother into letting you stay; it wasn't easy to explain how you just up and left."

"I can imagine, especially since I can't explain it myself. But then I'm crazy remember? Why don't we leave it at that?"

"That, my friend," agreed Daniel, "is the only way I can describe you. But that doesn't give my mother reason to trust you."

"No, I suppose not. But being crazy doesn't give me a lot of options, you know."

"I said it was the only way I could describe you. I didn't mean that I thought you were. There's something very weird about you, that's for sure. But I don't believe you're crazy."

"Well that's a small victory for me, then," said Michael. Then he pointed to the *chabako* and said, "Since I can't tell you the secrets of the tea set, maybe you can tell me."

"Actually, my knowledge of the tea set didn't begin until the night you dropped into my life."

"Really?"

"Oh, I knew it existed. I knew it held dishes for the Japanese Tea Ceremony, but that was all I knew or cared to know. It seems a rather feminine activity if you ask me." Michael felt Daniel's words as an insult and was getting ready to defend himself when Daniel continued. "I asked my mother where it came from after you disappeared and she told me the history of the set. It is a story that gave me pleasure and I find honor in its past."

Now we're getting somewhere, thought Michael. "And what is the story?" he asked.

"Just that it was made by an ancient ancestor. It has passed through the hands of my family for hundreds of years and it has great value. It dates back to the sixteenth century."

"That's four hundred years ago!" Michael was astonished and couldn't believe the tea set survived that many centuries.

"Not quite. Do the math," Daniel instructed.

"I did. It is the math of the future."

Daniel ignored Michael's remark and continued with his story.

"Anyway, my mother says the tea set was handed down to her through family on her mother's side. Someone named Takeya, who was originally a sword maker from Owari, made it. My mother said he was killed shortly after making this tea set."

"A sword maker? Why would someone who makes swords make a tea set? My grandmother has a beautiful set of samurai swords, I wonder if this guy, could have made them?"

"He's my ancestor, you idiot," Daniel said.

And mine, thought Michael silently.

"We own a set of fine samurai swords," Daniel told him. "And they might well have come from my illustrious ancestor. Who knows? I will ask my mother."

"Where are the swords now? Can I see them?" Michael wanted to see if they were the same swords he had wrapped so carefully in his grandmother's home.

"That's right. I keep forgetting there are certain things you pretend you know nothing about. When the FBI was confiscating "contraband" from all of us, my mother was wise enough to take the swords to the farm of a friend and bury them there. For the time being they are hidden and cannot be stolen from us."

Michael was glad, even though he would have liked to see the swords. For, if they had not been buried away somewhere, Michael's grandmother would probably not have them in her possession today. Or in 2002 anyway, he thought, because today his grandmother was actually only six years old.

"So how is Beth?" Michael asked.

"Beth?" Daniel repeated.

"Yes Beth, your sister."

"Beth is fine; she is too young to realize what is going on. She seems to think this is a big camp out or something," Daniel muttered absently.

Michael thought Daniel seemed a bit envious of Beth's innocence. It had shielded her from much of what had happened, until now. "Isn't she frightened by the fact that her grandfather has been shot and killed?" he asked Daniel.

"Now that you mention it, I guess that must have upset her. I never even thought of her and how she might feel, I have been so angry."

"I'm sure I would feel the same in your place," Michael said. He remembered what his grandmother had told him about how she'd been lucky to be a child at that time. So he said to Daniel, "You know, she's sheltered by childhood. She doesn't see things the way you do. She's too young to be aware of what's going on."

Daniel did not answer. Both boys sat in the silence as the wind blew in the distance.

With the wind, blew voices. Michael could hear bits of conversation beyond the garden. "What's going on outside?" he asked.

"It is the *Obon* Festival. The festival of the dead," Daniel answered. "It is a time when many of the old ones believe the souls of dead ancestors are supposed to return for three days. It gives my grandmother some comfort that grandfather died at the time we celebrate *Obon*."

"I thought you were Christian," Michael said.

"We are! It is like a Japanese All Soul's Day, okay? We say prayers in particular for anyone who has died in the previous year. It is believed they need more guidance to find their way. Grandmother eats like a bird, and she hoards little things from each meal to offer to Grandfather."

Michael gently laid his hand on Daniel's back and said, "What are we waiting for, then? Let's go."

"All right." Daniel left first, and Michael followed.

Since Daniel's family was Catholic, he followed the group of people entering the makeshift chapel. They were the last to enter and Michael and Daniel each dipped their fingers into the holy water font and crossed themselves. Daniel continued alone up the center of the chapel and knelt with his family. Michael remained in the rear. He too, knelt in the silence of the chapel, and prayed for his great-great-grandfather. When the service was over, he slipped outside before the rest and followed Daniel's group of people to a grave that held the first casualty of the camp. A rounded, wooden tombstone bore the words:

IN MEMORIAM
REQUIESCAT IN PACE
SHIRO ENDO
MAY 3, 1884 - July 15, 1942

Michael heard the voices of the family and moved into the distance, not wanting to be seen. He watched as the ancient customs blended with the faith they professed. His great-great-grandmother Endo approached the grave first. She knelt to place her little "treats" at the base of the tombstone, to honor her husband and feed his wandering spirit. Light from the lanterns shone on the many stalls in the center of the camp. Michael felt the spirit of his people enter his heart. And the spirits suddenly connected.

After praying over the grave, the mourners moved on to join other camp members taking part in the festival. Michael remained rooted some distance from the grave. Daniel walked towards him.

"Come on, surely you're going to join us? Have you never commemorated your grandmother or mother with prayers and such?" he asked.

Michael was struck with a new guilt. He had not. While he had missed the mother he couldn't remember, he'd never thought to offer prayers for her soul. He looked at the flickering lanterns and the lights and yearned to do just that.

Daniel shook his head at Michael's ignorance and said, "Just follow me."

As they approached, the lights illuminated the vibrantly dressed dancers swiveling to and fro. The graceful gestures made by each of them as they waved their fans spoke one message. Like water pouring from the pitcher to the glass, the movements were fluid. Michael drank them with delight. The beat of the *taiko* drums and the harmony of the *ondo* music made him, for just a moment; long to be a part of this place and time.

He had a glimpse of his mother, in the only way he knew her, laughing in the photo above the piano. Only now he saw her also as a spirit hungry for his prayers. He offered one for her that very moment. The first prayer he had said for his mother, and it was actually being offered before either of them were born.

"My grandfather loved to watch the *Bon Odori* dancers," Daniel said. "It's fitting he's buried during this time."

The festival was starting to wind down when Daniel led Michael back to the little hut he had shown him earlier. Once again, they entered on their knees.

Inside they knelt again before the *chabako*. Michael opened the door and gently removed the *chawan*. Daniel did not object.

Four hundred years, he thought. He looked around the little hut and wondered at the preparations Daniel had made. It had to be for the tea ceremony. Michael asked, "Why is the door so small?"

"The doorway is small because…" the words fell from his mouth. But his voice became a whisper from long ago, falling from the edge of the sky. His black T-shirt melted into the night. His face; the last of a vision Michael could see no more. And then he was gone into the thin air of the past.

CHAPTER FOUR

Michael could still feel a slight tingling in his legs. He waited for several moments before opening his eyes. Please, he thought, let me be home. Slowly, he inched them open. But he knew he wasn't home before his lashes had even touched his brow.

There were hundreds of stalls set up on the grounds around him, and a flurry of activity as men in vibrant colored kimonos hurried to and fro.

In the open stall nearest him, he saw an old man and heard him shout at a young boy standing before him. "Do not stand there idle! The moon shall have swallowed the sun and still you will not have achieved a portion of your task."

The man was speaking Japanese. But Michael understood his words. He also understood that this time, he had not only traveled through time, he had traveled through place. He was no longer in America. He was in Japan. His problems with time travel seemed to be getting worse rather than better. He was farther from home now than ever.

Michael remembered how some of his questions made him look crazy to Daniel. This time, he would be more careful. He would not so readily confess his problem. He would wait until the time was right. Hopefully, he would recognize the moment. And so he just sat and listened as the boy tried to appease the old man.

"What is it that you want me to do, honorable master?" The boy bowed before the man.

"Oh, curse the pigs that raised you, you simple-minded son of a sow. You have fashioned the entranceway too small! You want to make the great Hideyoshi crawl to enter and share tea?" The old man picked up a stick of bamboo and hit the boy on the shoulder. "Now go, quickly to my wagon and fetch more materials. Hideyoshi will enter my tea room with honor or you shall pay the price!"

The boy bowed repeatedly as he backed out of the stall. Only after he was outside did he turn and walk frontward. Michael got up and followed him.

"Hello," he said as he caught up to the boy.

The boy bowed towards Michael several times and said, "*Konnichiwa*, good afternoon! I am Thomas Kozaki."

"And I'm Michael…" he stopped himself just before saying Brogan. "What's going on here anyway?"

"Have you not heard? The great general, Toyotomi Hideyoshi is to attend a tea gathering."

"No, I'm not from around here," Michael answered cautiously.

"Ever since Lord Hideyoshi made this his feudal capital and had Osaka Castle built, tea ceremonies have become more popular.

"Lord Hideyoshi is quite taken with the Way of Tea. He obtains great pleasure in judging how it is presented by others," Thomas explained.

"Why was that man yelling at you?" Michael wanted to know.

"I work for him. I am helping to build his tea room."

"He's a real monster isn't he?"

"I will do as he asks. But he is wrong in what he orders. He knows nothing of *Chado*. The Way is not for proud men. The *nijiriguchi,* or entrance should be crawled through. It is best to bow when passing through this entrance. In bowing, we naturally lose our sense of self-importance and become humble. By crawling through the opening, a host and his guests enter another realm where they share a common fortune. No distinctions are made and they become

37

united. My master shall insult Lord Hideyoshi by trying to impress him."

Daniel's small door makes sense now, thought Michael. And remembering Daniel, Michael wished he could have thanked him. Now he was in Japan. But when was he here? He wondered what year it was in Japan. He didn't want Thomas to think he was crazy. He would have to ask his questions carefully.

"Are you from around here?" Michael asked.

"My family and I are natives of Ise. My father used to make fine bows for hunters. But it is his skill as a carpenter that has brought us to Osaka. You see, we are Christians and my father has helped to build convents and churches. The missionaries cannot pay so I try to get work to help my father."

"The missionaries?" Michael asked.

"Yes, the padres have taught me many things. And with the skills of my father, I have been lucky to find work here among the *chajin*."

"The *chajin?*" Michael felt a tremor of excitement flow through him simply at the recognition of the word for tea men.

"Yes, many of the *chajin* are kind and humble men. They are calm and content with a *wabi* state of mind."

"What is *wabi?*" Michael asked.

"*Wabi*," Thomas answered, "is finding beauty in the unadorned. My current master knows nothing of *wabi*. He is distressed easily."

"What does beauty have to do with being calm?" Michael still didn't understand all this talk about beauty and nature, and calmness and humility.

"You see the fallen petals of the cherry blossom?" Thomas pointed. "They remind us of the fleeting nature of this life. Jesus told us to consider the lilies of the field, how they grow; they toil not - neither do they spin. Even Solomon in all his glory was not arrayed like one of these."

Michael nodded to let Thomas know that he understood. And he decided then to try and stay close to Thomas. He was glad that these leaps into the past had at least paired him with boys close to his own age. He pinched himself hard, just to be sure that he wasn't dreaming. He winced in pain. He was awake all right, in another world.

"Thomas, could you use some help? I have nowhere to go and I need a place to stay. Would your father mind if I stayed with you?"

Thomas laughed good-naturedly. "We have no home to offer you here in Osaka. We too, are travelers. We are staying at the monastery. Don't worry. The padres will welcome you. They turn no one away."

And so, Michael helped Thomas. They removed the planks of wood that Thomas had cut for the *nijiriguchi*. Thomas recalculated the height his master desired and together the boys sawed the larger opening. Michael wiped beads of sweat from his forehead and wondered what Thomas would think if he could see the electric tools that carpenters used in his time.

When Thomas was satisfied that the sawed edges were smooth enough, they fashioned an entryway that a grown man could enter without bowing his head.

They were nearly through when Thomas said, "Are you hungry, as I am? Come, we will stop and eat." Michael followed him back to his master's wagon. A great pillar of steam rose from the caldron that hung above the campfire. Suddenly, Thomas turned and studied Michael. "You are dressed as a *gaijin*, foreigner."

"These are the only clothes I have," Michael said.

"I do not mind what you wear. But perhaps we should find something else before the others see you," he motioned for Michael to follow him to the other side of the wagon. Thomas rooted in the wagon for several moments and finally held up his findings. "This should do nicely," he said and handed Michael the roll of cloth. "You can change here," he said.

Unfolding the cloth, Michael found it was a thin kimono. He kicked off his shoes and pulled off his trousers. He kept his t-shirt on and slipped into the kimono. He tightened the sash and said, "Okay, I'm ready Thomas."

Thomas turned and studied him. The socks were still on his feet. Michael was in the process of slipping into his shoes when Thomas said, "Those will not do."

Michael knew he was right. Sneakers were not part of this world. Thomas again rooted through the wagon. This time he proudly produced a pair of straw sandals. "These go well with a kimono," he laughed. It occurred to Michael that Thomas was a happy sort. He knew that he would not be happy to live the life of Thomas. But he didn't worry that he would be here forever. After all, he had left the other pasts he had entered. The nagging question that remained was whether he would ever return to the future.

Thomas led the way back to the campsite. There were groups of men dotting the landscape. They sat on their haunches and shoveled the food with chopsticks into their mouths. An old man greeted Thomas, "*Konnichiwa*. I wondered if you were planning to eat today."

"Of course, Jiro. But I have been busy working."

Jiro looked from side to side before whispering, "No wonder you are too busy too eat. Those who work for Korin are lucky to have time to eat at all."

"I am fine, Jiro. Besides, I have found a friend to help me. This is Michael."

Jiro studied Michael for several moments. Then he picked up a wooden bowl from the basket at his feet and dished steaming noodles into it and handed it to Michael.

"A friend to Thomas is a friend to me," he said gruffly and handed Michael the bowl. He did the same for Thomas, but before passing the bowl to him, he brought it back over the caldron and added another portion. "Korin treats you miserably; I can at least see that he feeds you well."

Thomas grabbed a couple sets of chopsticks from the basket of utensils and Michael did the same. They found a spot to themselves in a grove of bamboo trees. The boys knelt and Michael was about to eat

40

when he saw that Thomas had settled the bowl in his lap and was bowing his head in prayer. He watched as Thomas slowly raised his fingers first to his forehead, and then crossed both shoulders in the sign of the cross.

It wasn't that Michael didn't want to pray. He just never thought of it when grown-ups weren't around to remind him. He followed Thomas' actions and crossed himself and whispered a prayer of his own. The boys commenced eating with gusto.

The flavor of the noodles was strange, yet good. Michael realized he was hungry. In between bites, Thomas told Michael about the journey he had made with his father.

"My mother remains at home with my little brothers. I miss them, but my father has done me a great honor by allowing me to accompany him."

When they were finished Thomas stood and said, "We must hurry if we want to make it back into the village before dark." They returned their bowls to Jiro and Thomas bid him good-bye, "See you tomorrow, Jiro."

"*Sayonara,* Thomas." Jiro smiled and waved.

The walk to the village didn't take too long, and Thomas filled the time with talk of his father and the missions. "This is the mission," Thomas said, as they approached a set of buildings. "You see my father's hand in much of the work here."

The church itself was not as large as the churches Thomas was used to, but the craftsmanship was excellent. Thomas led Michael to a smaller structure on the grounds. Michael stared in amazement at what he now knew was a teahouse. "I am a *dojuku,* a lay acolyte in training," he said proudly. "I will soon be an altar boy and serve at Holy Mass. I shall light the candles on the altar, and carry them in procession and during the solemn singing of the Gospel. Once I am finished with my training I will no longer work outside. Besides these duties, I will keep the mission teahouse in order at all times."

"I didn't realize the church was involved in *Chado,*" Michael replied.

"Oh yes," Thomas said. "Father Valignano, the superior of the Jesuits, ordered all their residences to have *chanoyu*. Many of the missionaries believe love for the tea ceremony tends to deepen their Christian faith. And so here in Osaka, the missionaries have achieved a pleasing harmony between Christianity and the tea."

"What is that," Michael asked, pointing to the small building a short distance before the teahouse.

"Come, I will show you," Thomas told him.

"This room serves as a storage area," Thomas told him as they entered the structure.

"You mean like a museum?" Michael said.

"It resembles the Imperial Repository, the *Shosoin*, in Japan's ancient city of Nara. The *Shosoin*, contains many treasures of Japanese history," Thomas explained.

Michael chided himself for speaking in modern terms. He wondered when the word 'museum' was coined. Thomas made no mention of the word, and continued his explanations as they walked into the wooden building that stood on stilts. "Here we store mostly items valued by Christians," he said.

Michael saw books, paintings, rosaries and chalices in various places throughout the room. A flash of red caught his attention. He saw lying on a low table, a pair of dragons enhancing the handle of a sword. Michael nearly ran to get a closer look. Just as he remembered, each dragon faced the other, as if ready to leap in combat. Just as he remembered, the dragon nearest the blade bore the haughty face of victory. The sword was unsheathed but the lacquered crimson scabbard rested beside the glistening blade.

Michael longed to tell Thomas, "This is my grandmother's sword!" He ached to tell someone. Instead he said, "What a magnificent sword."

"Yes, it was made by a great sword maker," Thomas told him. "But he never made another after this one."

"Why not?" Michael asked.

"Because he became a Christian. He vowed to God that he would no longer make instruments of violence. He gave the sword to the missionaries as a symbol that he was a man of peace. He told them that the blade had never been stained with blood and that he wished it to remain clean."

Michael's heart pounded in his chest. While the sword had not been the vehicle that transported him to the past, it was his only connection to his own life. If only he could touch it, maybe…

"Come, I want to show you the tearoom," Thomas said, gently tugging at his arm, pulling him away from the sword.

Michael followed, but vowed to himself that he would come back as soon as possible. He would touch the sword and see if it could take him home.

Michael crawled through the *nijiriguchi* after Thomas. The room was nearly empty but for a small stand of utensils. Thomas went to the stand, picked up an item, then turned and showed it to Michael.

"This was given to my family by the great sword maker," Thomas laughed. "You see how the great God of heaven likes a joke now and then? Kosuma Takeya, greatest of all sword makers, now fashions these."

Michael stared at the object Thomas held. He felt a tingling and it wasn't just in his legs.

Thomas went on, "Kosuma Takeya was baptized by the Jesuits and works here as a catechist with the Franciscans in Osaka. This was the first tea set he made after finishing his last set of swords."

Thomas turned the *chawan* over and read the brush strokes on the bottom, "Put down the sword - put on the armor of God." Michael took the *chawan* from Thomas' outstretched hand.

He stared at the strange Japanese characters on the bottom. They revealed the conversion of the individual who painted them. The swords and the tea set were connected. The same man had made them both and he lived in the sixteenth century! Michael felt as if he were about to faint. He slowly eased to the kneeling position, resting back on his heels. He then looked at the *chawan* in his hand. The dark amber glaze was the same. But the small crosses were much brighter around the rim. The tingling settled in his legs, warning him of what was to come.

CHAPTER FIVE

Michael was still in a seated position with his eyes closed. Funny, he didn't remember having closed them. Just moments before, he had dropped to his knees with the realization that he had traveled centuries in time. But he had not closed his eyes. Or had he? He made up his mind to pay closer attention to every movement he made when holding the *chawan*.

He thought it odd that such attention was also a necessary component in *Chado*. He hesitated before opening his eyes. He didn't hope to be in his own time. Somehow, he knew that he wouldn't be. While he wasn't sure what this time traveling was all about, he had a certain sense that he was not finished yet.

And so he opened his eyes. He was sitting next to an earthen wall. He shivered, for it was very cold. There was about an inch of crisp snow covering the ground. He looked up and saw high in the sky above him, the large multi-storied tower of a Japanese castle.

The earthen wall he was sitting near looked as if it surrounded the castle and was dotted with small openings that looked to the outside. Michael got up and went to one of the openings and looked out. He saw a maze of moats, walls and courtyards. He was standing in the center of a labyrinth, which was a Japanese castle compound.

For the first time in his travels, he had arrived in a place empty of people. And while he was longing to figure out how to get home, he could not help but be fascinated with this place. The architecture of the castle, even from the outside, was magnificent. Vast, round beams formed the roofs of each structure. Even the low, earthen wall was crowned with the same symmetrical design.

Suddenly, he heard low voices. The voices were speaking in Japanese, but as before, he could understand them.

"*Santa Maria Sama,*" a man's voice called to the Virgin Mary.

"Pray for us," answered a chorus of voices.

Michael walked in the direction of the voices. They were coming from a building within the maze where he stood.

"*O Yasu Sama no Yofu,*" this was the name for St. Joseph, the adoptive father of Our Lord.

"Pray for us," they repeated again.

Michael tried peering in the small window but it was difficult, as the entire window was studded with spikes and crisscrossed with iron bars. Still, he saw him right away. There, just below the window, knelt Thomas.

"Psst, Thomas," he whispered. "Thomas, it's me, Michael."

Thomas turned and looked at him. Michael gasped in horror. The entire left side of Thomas's face was bloody. The blood had run down his shoulder and his kimono was stained. Michael did not want to see, but could not stop from scanning his friend's face for the source of his wound. His gaze landed where Thomas's ear used to be. Michael's stomach lurched at the sight of the wound. His ear had been severed.

"What's happened to you Thomas?" he screamed.

"Shush," Thomas said softly. "Don't let them hear you. They will capture you too."

"Is this a prison?" he asked.

"It is a prison for us," Thomas answered.

Michael looked at the others who had been praying and were now looking at Michael from inside. Each of them bore a wound like Thomas. Each of them had had their left ear sliced from their head. And each of them was shackled to the other with iron manacles around their left ankles. The chain between the manacles was about three feet in length.

"Why have they done this to you? What have you done?" his stomach continued to lurch and he swallowed hard to keep from vomiting right in front of them.

"Because we are Christians," Thomas said. Then he smiled and added proudly, "We are to be crucified, like our Blessed Master!"

"How can you smile at a time like this? Do you want to die?" Michael wondered how Thomas could be so calm. "You should be angry, if nothing else! This is an outrage!"

The man shackled closest to Thomas put his arm gently around the boy's shoulders. "Is this the young friend you told me about, Thomas?"

"Yes, Father. He too, bears the name Michael." Then, bending low at the waist in a ceremonial bow, Thomas said, "Michael, this is my most honorable *Otosan,* Father."

"Uh… it's nice to meet you," Michael answered. He couldn't believe they were actually exchanging pleasantries from inside a prison, with blood trickling from their wounds.

"What kind of torture is this?" Michael couldn't lower his voice, though he tried. Even as he tried to whisper, his voice was shrill, "What have they done to you?"

"We have been spared our right ears," Thomas said. "Most prisoners loose both ears after being captured." Thomas pointed to a man several lengths down the chain from where he stood. "To punish Kosuma Takeya for giving up his trade as a sword maker, the guards used his untainted sword to slash the bodies of his fellow Christians. They used his work as the tool of torture. But he has remained strong in his faith."

"You said he put away his swords to put on the armor of God," Michael cried. "How can God let this happen?"

At that, one of the men came forward, "I am Kosuma Takeya," he said. Michael looked at his ancestor. He studied the calm, bloodstained face. "The Heavenly Father has not left us unarmed. We now wear the helmet of salvation and we carry the sword of the Spirit," the old man bowed low and crossed himself as he spoke the name of the Holy Ghost.

Too late, Michael saw the guards walking towards him. One was very short, the other, tall and fat as a sumo wrestler. The short one grabbed him by the arm and, turning to the other said, "What have we here? Another Christian?"

"No!" Michael shouted angrily. He tried to wriggle away, but it was no use.

The larger guard laughed and said, "What a business we are sending to the cross maker. This makes twenty-seven." He jerked Michael's other arm from the small man's grasp and dragged him around the side of the building with ease.

The small guard struggled to lift the heavy crossbeam from the iron slots across the door. When it was lifted, the sumo wrestler thrust it open with his great hip and threw Michael inside. Michael fell against a young boy and he, along with the boy and two men shackled to him, fell in a heap to the floor. With a hearty laugh the guard shut the door and Michael heard the beam thud in place.

As he fell, his weight caused the shackles to dig deep into the boy's tender ankle, breaking the skin. Michael grew woozy. He swallowed against the vomit but his fear was stronger than pride and he retched in front of the others.

He was aware that the group of Christians had moved as one to lift him from the mess he'd made. The man at the end of the chain clawed at the earth with his fingernails, then tried to cover the stench with the dirt.

The men in the middle of the chained group lifted his body and laid him beneath the window.

Michael remembered that he had always shamed his father with his fear. His mind traveled to a

48

moment from his own time. His father had learned he had skipped school after being called a "Jap" by a group of boys.

"Running away solves nothing, Michael," he'd said, as if it were so simple.

"Give me a break, Dad. You don't know what it's like to be me."

"You're right, I don't. But I do know that you must learn to face your problems. Otherwise, you will never grow up. Be a man, be a man, be it ever so painful."

Michael hated the way his dad peppered every argument with little sayings. He seemed to think clever lines ended the argument in his favor.

Michael could almost smell the scrambled eggs his father had slapped on the table in front of him that day. How sick they'd made him.

"Instead of being so angry about not blending in, why not look at what makes you proud about being different."

"Easy for you to say," Michael answered.

His dad sat down across from him with his own plate. He grabbed the bottle of hot sauce from the middle of the table and dumped it over his eggs. He looked at Michael before taking that first bite and said, "Those samurai swords you're always talking about; the men who owned them looked like you. But they were not ashamed of it," he then lifted the forkful of eggs into his mouth.

Michael's stomach turned for the second time. He swallowed hard. His weak stomach had always been a pathetic sign to his father that he was immature.

"You can't take pride in an heirloom when you are ashamed of the ancestry that created it. Only when you realize that - will you be worthy of owning them."

Anger churned the fear in his belly. "I never said I was ashamed!"

"No, but you've made it clear that looking like your ancestors makes you feel un-American."

"It's not me Dad! It's the way everyone else sees me." His father, finished by this time with breakfast, got up and put his plate in the dishwasher. Then he walked over and placed his large American hands on Michael's shoulders.

"Michael, they only see what you show them. I hope someday you'll learn that only you can determine who you are. The samurai were men who followed a code of honor. They met their difficulties and challenges with a sense of pride. Each time people see you shy away from your own image, you're providing them with the shame they smear you with."

Michael remembered how he had run from the table to the bathroom. He had always thrown up when he was upset. His body rejected what his mind could not digest. But back then; it was his own misery that made him sick.

Now, a shiver of fear ran through him and he couldn't stop shaking. He sat up and leaned his body firmly against the wall. The bloodied faces around him seemed so calm compared to his own fear. He couldn't be like them! How stupid to accept so easily such a terrible fate.

"Can't somebody stop this?" he asked. "How can they do this just because of your beliefs? Why?"

One of the men, whom Thomas introduced as Paul Miki, tried to explain. "The Shogun, Hideyoshi, has commanded our death. No one can stop it now."

Michael looked at Thomas who stood nodding his head in agreement. "But you said this Hideyoshi fellow followed the Chado. How can he do this if he is a man of the Tea?"

"Chado in and of itself does not transform a cruel man into a kind one. And you must know that Hideyoshi, while once a friend to Christians, is most concerned for power. The San Felipe Incident has threatened his domain."

"The San Felipe Incident?" Michael asked.

"Ah, you have not heard of the great Spanish galleon that ran aground off the coast and sought refuge in the port of Urado?"

"No," answered Michael.

"Hideyoshi seized the cargo of the ship and the captain was very angry. We still do not know if the

Spaniard told a lie to the Shogun or if the story is only slander. But the rumor spread that the captain bragged that the empire of Spain could conquer Japan, through first sending missionaries as spies.

"Hideyoshi is now furious and extremely suspicious. He has ordered the missionaries and Christians to be captured and crucified."

At this the smallest of the group, made his way over to Michael. "You shall not be crucified with us." His bright eyes and intelligent face lent truth to his words. But Michael was still frightened.

"How can you know what will happen to me?" he asked.

"You are not of our time. Our Lord will not take you from the world before you are born into it."

He's only a boy thought Michael, how can he know all this? Then he asked him, "How old are you?"

"I am the youngest here, twelve years in age. My name is Louis Ibaragi. The missionaries in Kyoto, where we were captured, baptized me only ten months ago." A broad smile lit up his face.

Paul Miki looked with great fondness on Louis. He said to Michael, "Louis is young indeed. But he sees with a pure heart blessed by God. You can trust his words as truth."

Michael spent the next few moments listening to the gentle whispers among the men. He sat in silence next to Thomas wondering what was going to happen, then Thomas spoke, "Do not worry over us, Michael. Death is the beginning of life."

"I hate when you talk like that," Michael told him. "What do you know of death? You have never died." He couldn't help being angry. To him life was precious. How could they act as if their death was of no consequence? "It's that samurai garbage right?" he demanded rather than asked. "You think it is bushido? You die and it doesn't matter?"

"Do not confuse the way of the warrior with the bushido of the Christian samurai, Michael. There are differences."

"Such as?" Michael goaded his friend.

"A pagan samurai will commit *seppuku,* ritual suicide, for an ungodly master, because he has sworn him loyalty. The Christian samurai honors all of life, but shall gladly die at a pagan's hand to be born again to life with God."

"Either way, you're dead," Michael said. "Why can't you just go back the way you were? Go along with these men." Michael knew how the Japanese revered their ancestors, so he tried that. "Your ancestors, they were not Christian."

Thomas looked thoughtful and said, "While it is true that many Japanese are not Christians because they do not want to walk a path different from their ancestors, I walk the path of Christ. Faith is for all of us, a gift apart from a man's country.

"In following the Christian path, I have walked in the company of saints. We Japanese must first walk this new path, if we have any hope that future generations can walk the way of a Christian ancestor."

At that moment they heard voices of the guards approaching. Thomas looked at Michael and his eyes were filled with his urgent plea, "*Dozo,* please Michael, I ask of you a great favor." For the first time Michael saw Thomas as apprehensive.

"Sure, Thomas," Michael answered. And yet, he was concerned at what Thomas may ask. He did not have the courage of Thomas, nor his faith. He was stunned that Thomas was going to be crucified. "But I think your father should tell you to apostatize."

Thomas sucked in his breath but Michael went on, "Doesn't he care what happens to you?"

"He cares, Michael."

"I think it is disgraceful. How can a father stand by and watch his son tortured and killed?"

"He knows I am honored to die as he will, in the service of Our Lord," Thomas clasped Michael's hand and said, "You will do this favor?" Michael swallowed hard and nodded.

"One of the guards at Mihara Castle, where we were held for a time, was sympathetic to the Christians. He smuggled writing material to me and I have written a letter to my mother. I am asking you to see that she gets it." Thomas reached inside his kimono and pulled out the folded rice paper. Just as Michael reached out to take it, they heard the heavy beam being lifted from the door of their prison. Thomas' father quickly plucked it from Thomas as the sumo wrestler entered. Hiding it in the sleeve of his kimono, he pretended to be scratching his arm.

"Time to move on," the guard ordered. "You are nearing the end of your journey." The twenty-three men and three young boys quietly followed the man outside.

Thomas silently turned to Michael and whispered, "Oh please, see that she gets this, if nothing else." From inside his kimono he pulled out an object and thrust it swiftly into Michael's hand. Michael hurriedly thrust it into the sleeve of his kimono as Thomas' father had done.

Outside, Michael saw streets lined with people on either side. Not being chained to them, Michael managed to slip away from the Christians and join the crowd of spectators. His emotions were torn into relief at his escape, and shame that he was running from his friend. Still, he did not follow Thomas and the others. He just stood there and watched as they walked over the horizon. The final image of them was the blood red stains their footprints left in the snow.

He slumped to the ground. Remembering the object Thomas had given him, he reached in his sleeve and pulled it out. He held again the *chawan* with the tiny crosses. His legs began to tingle and his eyes grew heavy.

CHAPTER SIX

Michael knew that he would soon be somewhere else. Ever since the tea ceremony with his grandmother, he had traveled through time whenever he held the *chawan*. He had always given in to the process, hoping each time he opened his eyes he would find himself back home.

Except this time was different. Of course, Michael still wanted to go home. But he couldn't run out on Thomas and the others. He wanted desperately to know what had happened to them. So while his legs were still tingling, he struggled against the desire to relax. He forced his eyes to open before they had a chance to completely close.

He felt the cold, snow covered ground and he saw that it was still stained with the bloodied footprints of Thomas and his friends. The *chawan* was still in his hands. He secured it in the large pocket inside his kimono and stood.

The crowd that had lined the streets earlier was already several yards ahead. They, too, must have been anxious to learn the fate of the Christians. Michael followed them.

With each step, his heartbeat quickened. It flapped rapidly in his chest, fluttering like the wings of a frightened bird. And yet, he could not run away. He was closing the gap between himself and his friend.

Michael heard a voice cry out above the crowd, "Oh Lord, open my lips." It was Paul Miki. After he intoned these words his companions answered, "And our mouths will proclaim Thy praise!"

Michael shivered, and a puzzling peace entered his soul. The fluttering in his chest faded and the words that fell from the lips of the Christians calmed him somehow. Several people in the crowd began to answer the prayer also.

"Exult in His presence and serve Him with joy," Paul's voice did not waver.

"Let us come before the Lord and proclaim our thanks."

"Know that the Lord is God. He made us."

"We are His people, the sheep of His flock."

Michael knew the prayer was true. Though Thomas and the others were being led to further torture and perhaps even death, they were truly the people of God.

"Cry out His praises as you enter His gates, fill His courtyards with songs."

"Proclaim Him and bless His name for the Lord is our delight."

"His mercy lasts forever, His faithfulness through all the ages."

While some people in the crowd continued to pray, others cried out to the guards, "*Jihi*, mercy!" One old woman ran beyond the guards and fell to the ground at little Louis' feet. "*Osanago*! He is but a little child. An infant to this life," she wept.

"Do not cry for me, ancient one," Louis said to her. "I am ready to go before Our Lord. My soul is at peace, my heart is full of joy."

There was a hush over the crowd, for they had reached their destination. They stood on top of a wide hill overlooking the sea. The hill had been prepared before their arrival. Twenty-six crosses had been prepared for the Christians. Three of them were small. They were crosses for children.

Louis asked softly, "Which one is mine?"

A samurai pointed to the smallest one and Louis tried to run towards it. He nearly made it before the shackle on his ankle brought him down. He fell to the ground. He pushed the palms of his hands against the earth and braced himself to rise. Thomas bent and grasped him under the arm. "You are an impatient one. No reason to hurry, Louis. Our day has finally come!" He pulled the boy to his feet and smiled at him.

Louis looked at Thomas with admiration. Michael saw that these Christians shared a love for one another that would bind them beyond death.

Abruptly, a large guard tromped heavily towards the prisoners and began to undo the shackles at their feet.

Thomas gave Louis' shoulder an affectionate squeeze just as they were separated. Michael watched in horror as a guard grabbed each of his friends and began fixing them to their crosses. They were not nailed, but fastened by their hands, feet, and necks with iron rings. A rough rope was tightly knotted around their waists.

The missionaries were placed in the center, the crosses of their Christian followers flanking each side. These crosses were different from the crucifixes Michael had imagined. There were beams not only in place for the arms to be secured, but also for the legs. An additional beam extended beyond the others, and the men were straddled upon it. Paul Miki was too short for the cross they had fashioned for him. They tried to stretch his legs to meet the rings on the lower leg beams. Michael saw Paul's jaw muscles tighten as they strained his body, but he did not cry out.

And then the guards were finished. Seeing his friends so near to death, Michael's peace evaporated. He felt as if he couldn't breathe. His heart began to pound, and there was something bouncing back and forth in his head. It was a word. One small word. But the force of it crashed into his brain. He shouted the word, "No! No!" His cries mingled with those of the crowd. While some wept in agony, others tempted the Christians to renounce their faith and save their lives.

Michael continued to shout, "No, please God, no!" And then, in unison the crosses were lifted on high. Twenty-six stood before the crowd and as one, were thumped into the holes that had been dug for them. Michael felt the thud of the crosses meeting the earth, and saw the waves of pain that shot through the bodies that hung on them.

A woman next to him began to weep loudly, crying, "Anthony! *Sochi,* my son!" A man with sad eyes stood beside her and took hold of her and held her close to him. Michael saw that the tears of the mother tore at the boy. "I love you, Mother. I love you, most honorable Father," he shouted to them from his cross. His voice, faltered just a moment, then rose to a crescendo as the voices of all twenty-six joined with his to sing, "Oh saving Victim, open wide - the gate of heaven to man below.

"Our foes press on from every side, Thine aid supply - Thy strength bestow."

Some of those in the crowd began to sing also. Through tears of grief even Anthony's parents, in the front row, took up the refrain, "All praise and thanks to Thee ascend, oh grant us life that shall not end - in our true native land with Thee."

The word, "No!" had stopped echoing in his head. Instead Michael found the words of their song lodged in his throat. Yet, the bloodied faces of his friends displayed no sadness. Though their bodies were battered and bruised and their blood had dried and caked to their cheeks, an amazing splendor spread from their souls and washed over the crowd. Michael stood, transfixed as the faith of his friends surged over him, tugging like an ocean tide.

The guards separated into two groups. The first formed a barrier between the crosses and the crowd; the second stood ready at the foot of each cross, pulling their long lances from the scabbards at their sides. The end of each lance was fitted with a sharp, glistening blade. One of the guards pulled off the decree of death that had been fastened to his blade.

"Silence!" he ordered. "I read now the sentence of death!" He threw his loud voice as hard as he could over the crowd. "As these men came from the Philippines under the guise of ambassadors, and chose to stay in Miyako preaching the Christian law, which has been severely forbidden, it has been decreed that they be put to death, together with the Japanese who have accepted that law."

Paul Miki waited until the guard had finished speaking. He struggled to straighten himself upon his cross. He looked out into the crowd and Michael felt as though he was looking directly at him. "All of you who are here, please, listen to me." Even the air stilled as if to wait for his words.

"I did not come from the Philippines. I am Japanese by birth and a brother of the Society of Jesus. I have committed no crime, and the only reason I am being put to death is that I have been teaching the doctrine of Our Lord Jesus Christ. This I will continue to do until my last breath. And I thank God that it is for this reason I am about to die."

Michael could see that it was becoming more and more difficult for Paul to speak. Still he continued. "The Christian law commands that we forgive our enemies and those who have wronged us. I say here and now, that I forgive all who took part in my death. I do not hate any of you. I pray that my blood will fall as that of a fruitful rain on all of my Japanese brethren."

Michael's face streamed with tears. But through them he caught sight of Kosuma Takeya, his ancestor. From his cross, the sword maker looked straight at Michael and said, "Walk always the way of Christ and honor shall be yours at the end."

And then Paul Miki raised his eyes to heaven and said, "Lord, into Thy hands I commend my spirit. Come to meet us, ye Saints of God…"

With a guttural yell the guards began thrusting their blades into the hearts of the men and boys. The warm blood gushed forth from their bodies, melting the snow, painting red rivers on the hill of Nishizaka. There was so much blood that Michael thought it must surely have flowed from the crosses of the Christians to the Nagasaki streets. Michael looked up and saw Kosuma Takeya's eyes close as his head slumped forward.

Screams rose from the crowd. Michael ran to Thomas, who was being speared at the other end of the line. The throng of people grew thick around him and he had to fight to make his way. Even though Michael knew that his friend was dead, he needed to say good-bye.

Before he could reach Thomas, who had been crucified on the twentieth cross, one of the guards rammed him with his club. Michael heard a crack near his rib cage. He was stunned a bit, but not in severe pain. He rubbed his side and felt something broken. Oh no, it couldn't be! He reached inside the kimono and pulled out the broken bits of the *chawan*. It was beyond repair. Would he never return to his own time? The broken bits fell from his fingers. He slumped to his knees and tried to gather each piece. He wanted so badly to cry. He felt completely helpless and alone. Yet he knew that the twenty-six souls that had just left this world had not cried as they faced torture and death.

He knew he didn't have their strength. But he was no longer the fearful boy he had been when he first met them.

The crowd continued to surge against him, trying to reach the bodies of the martyrs. A woman was hit and fell to the ground beside him. It was Anthony's mother. "Are you all right?" he asked.

"My son has been put to death," she said simply.

"I know. I am sorry," Michael said.

Her husband reached out for her and said, "Come, we will pray with the others." The couple approached the area where many had already fallen to their knees. The guards wouldn't let them close enough to touch their loved ones, but many were tearing bits of cloth from their kimonos and soaking them in the pools of blood.

He looked past the sword maker, past the many crosses of the dead. He saw that Thomas' father had died on the fourth cross. Louis and Anthony were right next to one another on the ninth and tenth crosses.

Thomas had been far removed from them on cross number twenty. He had not even been permitted to die next to his father or the other boys, Michael thought. He wondered if Thomas had looked for him in the crowd before he breathed his last. But he had been at the other end of the crosses when the lance had pierced Thomas' heart. Not even he was near Thomas when he died.

"Ah, this broken *chawan* is like ours," he heard someone say. A woman knelt beside him and helped him to pick up the shattered bits of clay.

"You mean to say this is not the only one?" Michael asked. He wondered if the other pieces held the same power to send him back and forth through time.

The woman pointed to the man who hung upon the second cross. "Kosuma Takeya, the sword maker, he was my brother. He made four of these *chawan*. They were his last pieces before he was captured along with Father Martin."

Placing his hand on the woman's shoulder Michael said, "I'm so sorry." He longed to tell her who he was, to tell her that they were connected by blood.

Instead he moved away from the woman, not even waiting to learn if he could hold her *chawan* in his hands. He walked the row of dead martyrs until he stood as close to Thomas' cross as the guards would allow.

"Good-bye my friend," he whispered to Thomas. Then he dropped to his knees and began to pray.

The martyrdom of
St. Thomas Kozaki and Companions

CHAPTER SEVEN

Kneeling in the snow near the twenty-six crosses, Michael prayed without words. His mind was empty of language or expression. His heart was beating; no, it was bursting, with the conviction that he was in the presence of God.

He prayed without words because words were not sufficient. A mantle of holiness covered the hill. And for just a moment, sanctity flushed away the flimsy words from his soul.

He felt pain in his hands, but the word, "ouch," never reached his lips. Opening his palms from the praying position, he saw blood running through his fingers.

The broken bits of the *chawan*, forgotten for those few moments, had sliced into his flesh. Michael watched as his blood fell to the ground, blending with the blood of the martyrs.

"Here, let me help you," it was the sword maker's sister. She picked the broken bits from his wound. Producing a small square of blue satin from her cloth kimono bag, she wrapped the pieces and placed the bundle back in her bag. Then, she withdrew a second cloth and wiped the blood from his hands.

"Come with me. It is over now, we must return to our homes." Michael got up and followed her without speaking.

She led him down the road to the village. They walked in silence past many others who were returning from the martyrs' hill.

It wasn't until they entered the doorway of a small, thatched roof hut that Michael found his voice. "Why are you helping me?"

"What else would you have me do?" the woman asked sadly. Then she said, "*Dozo*, please, sit." And Michael folded his legs and sat on the floor.

She knelt at the *hibachi* in the middle of the room to heat a kettle of water. Using a cloth, she carried the hot kettle to where Michael sat. She put it down and, taking the cloth, ripped two narrow strips from it. She dipped the remaining cloth in the water and wrung it out. Wiping his hands with the hot cloth, she said, "What we have witnessed has changed us forever. But it must be a change for good, or our loved one dies in vain, does he not?" Her eyes penetrated his and Michael felt she could read his every thought. She unwrapped a bundle and removed a pot that held some sort of paste. It was the color of seaweed and smelled terrible. She rubbed it between her fingers and then wiped it over his cuts.

"But it is too awful," Michael tried to explain. "I mean – Thomas, Anthony and Louis were only boys. It just isn't right!"

The old woman smiled a smile of sadness. She wrapped Michael's hand with one of the narrow strips of cotton, and then repeated the process with his other hand.

"It is impossible to have known God, to have tasted His heavenly gift, and turn away from our fellow man. *Shikata ga nai,* it does not matter about fair," she said.

Michael watched as she bound his wounds and he ached for his father and grandmother.

The woman made a bed of quilts for Michael and told him to rest. He lay on the bedding and exhaustion poured over him. His eyes grew heavy as he watched her clear away the material she had used to treat his wounds. I never asked her name, he thought. But he was so tired.

She was still busy as his eyes closed. Was he dreaming or did she bring him a bowl of tea? He felt the warmth of the liquid as it touched his lips. When he opened his eyes to take the bowl, he saw the neat, tiny crosses lining the familiar rim of the amber *chawan.* He drank of the tea and then he closed his eyes in sleep.

He heard noises as he slept. Faint at first, the noises grew gradually louder. Michael stretched his arms and rubbed his eyes with his fists. The roughness of the cotton bandages scratched his face. But there was no pain from his wounds.

He opened his eyes and saw a young boy, about five or six years old sitting next to him. The boy was holding a cricket cage. It was finely crafted from twigs and a sheath of bamboo shoots and resembled a country cottage. The noise Michael had heard was the singing of the crickets inside the cage.

"Mother, he is awake," the boy shouted.

A pretty young woman entered the room. "You have returned from the land of sleep. We were worried about you."

Michael looked around for the old woman. She wasn't there. Then, he noticed that the room itself was different. There was no *hibachi* in the center of the floor. The blankets he was covered with were of a different color. He looked at the bandages the old woman had applied. Prying them loose, he uncovered his hands. He was not surprised when he saw they were healed. He was, again, in another time.

"How long have I been here?" he asked.

"Since *kanashimi no hairi.*" Michael understood the strange Japanese words, but *kanashimi no hairi,* which meant, "entering into sorrow", confused him.

"You mean, sorrow for the martyrs?" he asked.

The little boy and the woman looked at each other and then at Michael. "Go, Ichiro" the woman said to the boy, "Tell your father."

"Yes, Mother." The boy scrambled to his feet and ran out the door, taking his crickets with him. The air grew heavy with silence. The woman looked at him and said, "You are *Kakure Krishitan*?"

64

"Hidden Christian?" Michael was puzzled by her words. "I am a Christian, yes. But I have not been hiding."

She opened a lacquer box and pulled something from it. "These *tamoto kami,* sleeve gods, were found under the sleeve of your kimono." She handed them to Michael and he saw that they were small crosses cut from paper. "We knew when we saw them that you were a *Kakure Krishitan.*"

Michael didn't know what she meant by *Kakure,* hidden, and he had no idea where the sleeve gods had come from. The old woman must have slipped them in his kimono while he slept.

Then, voices were heard at the door. Ichiro ran through as soon as it opened. "Slow down, Ichiro," said his mother.

"But Mother, Honorable Father has good news!" A man entered the room, behind Ichiro. He placed his hand on the boy's shoulder and said, "Slow down little one." Then he said to his wife, "He is excited, Yuko. I do indeed have news."

Yuko smiled and said, "Then we both have news, my husband." And she turned to look at Michael. Her husband did the same.

"I am Peter. I see you have met my family. What is your name and how did you come to be here?"

"My name is Michael, and I'm not sure how I came here. The last thing I remember is falling asleep. When I woke up, here I was."

"What a sleep you have had then," Peter laughed aloud. He looked to his wife and said, "Let us eat and I shall tell you of my news." He motioned for Michael to come with them.

At the table, the family bowed their heads and Peter recited a prayer. Yuko passed a serving bowl of rice around the table.

Peter then told of his news. "A *Bateren,* a priest, has come to Nagasaki!" Yuko gasped and looked sharply at her husband.

"*Dozo,* please, Yuko. It is true. I have seen him with my own eyes."

"How did you learn of this?" Yuko asked. "You have not asked questions publicly have you?"

"I have spoken only among the *Kakure Krishitan*. Perhaps we are finally to be blessed after so long."

Michael could remain silent no longer. "What are you talking about? You speak of "Hidden Christians" and talk as if you haven't seen a priest before in Nagasaki."

Peter said, "Since the ban on Christianity we have had to remain hidden from authorities. We have lived faithful to the memory of our ancestors, who died for Christ centuries ago. I am a catechist. My home is honored to house the *nandogami*."

He explained that the *nandogami* were closet gods, hidden from the authorities, but close at hand for the faithful. Peter rose and went to the closet. He brought six lacquer boxes back to the table. Handling the objects reverently, he opened the first box saying, "These are *gozensama*."

Michael caught his breath. Inside, beneath a woodblock print of Christ on the cross, was a scroll with a painting of twenty-six crosses bearing the bodies of twenty-three men and three boys. Peter continued with his explanations, but Michael was barely listening. He forced himself to look away from the picture of his friends and tried to pay attention as Peter returned the last item, a small metal statue of the Blessed Virgin, to the box.

He opened the second box. In it was a cloth bag. Peter opened the bag and gently emptied it of sixteen small pieces of wood. "These are *ofuda*," he said.

Each block of wood was etched with a cross, a number from one to five, and Japanese writing on the front. On the back, the Japanese characters indicated joyful *(oyorokobi)*, sorrowful *(okanashimi)*, or glorious *(gororiya-sama)*. The sixteenth piece had the joyful symbol and the word, amen.

"These blocks represent the fifteen mysteries of the Holy Rosary," Peter said.

Michael knew that Catholics prayed the Rosary with beads, strung together. Each mystery, or decade of beads, focused on a point in the life of Christ and His Blessed Mother. The *ofuda* was the Rosary in disguise.

Each box contained items that were important to the people and their faith. One held a vial of holy water they called, San Juan-sama. Peter explained that the Christians treasured these items as they lived their faith in secret.

The fifth box held *omaburi*. Inside it, were smaller boxes of fine quality, containing pieces of paper cut in the shape of a cross. Michael thought it looked like the container that held the Sacred Host the priest had brought to his mother as she lay dying.

I've remembered something, he thought. I've remembered something about my mother!

Peter was saying, "Each year we are forced to trample the *fumi,* a sacred Christian image. We pray in our hearts as we trod on our God. This we do to remain hidden. We have been without the *Bateren* for too long. We have been subjected to the tactics of the Christian Suppression Office without mercy. Were you spared of these things?"

"No," Michael said solemnly. "I have witnessed the murder of my friends."

"Then you know that we have carried on in secret. We have preserved the faith, hidden, for more than 200 years. And now, there is a *Bateren,* a priest, in Nagasaki! A great Cathedral has been built to honor the 26 martyrs."

"A cathedral!" Michael and Yuko cried in unison.

"Yes, it has been named, *"Oura Cathedral",* it is the Church of the 26 martyrs." Michael thought again of the twenty-six as he had last seen them, hanging on their crosses.

Long after Yuko had cleared away the meal, they talked. Ichiro finally fell asleep in Peter's lap. He picked him up and put him to bed. Then they spoke in whispers about the plans for the next day.

"We are going as a group into Nagasaki. We are going to approach the *Bateren.*" Michael listened, but he asked questions too.

"There is so much I do not know. I have spent much time on my own," he told Peter.

"The Holy Virgin has stood in our midst," Yuko said.

"Yes," agreed Peter, "but we have lost many through the centuries. In the *Shimbara* Rebellion thousands of Christians were killed rather than surrender. We lost 37,000 Christians and farmers combined, when Hara castle fell to shogunate forces in 1638. It has been said that many men, women and children were decapitated, their heads placed around the surrounding field. That siege lasted three months." Yuko made the sign of the cross and shook her head.

Peter continued, "During the final month of the siege, the Christians fired hardly any bullets. They chose instead, to melt them for crosses rather than to attack the enemy. They carried banners with Portuguese inscriptions such as "Louvada seia o Santissimo Sacramento" (Praised be the most Holy Sacrament). To this day, crosses, along with rosaries and bronze icons can be found in the ash and ruins.

"The rebels were starving near the end and the ammunition they had left was not enough. They had only barley and seaweed to eat."

Yuko said, "Many farmers joined the Christians at Shimbara. During that time, the authorities were forcing the farmers to turn over the bulk of their crops. Those who refused were forced to wear *mino,* coats made of straw, and set afire. The authorities laughed as the victims writhed in pain. They referred to this as *mino odori,* raincoat dancing.

"The farmers knew the Tokugawa shogunate was persecuting Christians. Crucifixion was a common form of punishment, as was being boiled alive or left to suffocate over a burning pit. And so the farmers joined the Christian rebellion at *Shimbara.* At the end, it was said the farmers performed as Christians and died in prayer."

"How many years ago did this happen?" Michael asked, though he knew Peter had said 1638. He congratulated himself on inconspicuously finding out the present year.

"Over two hundred years ago…" Peter rubbed his chin, "Let's see, it is now 1865… that means it was two hundred and…" he scratched his head.

Yuko laughed, "Shall I find the abacus, Husband?" she asked with a twinkle in her eye.

"It was two hundred and twenty seven years ago. Abacus my foot!" Peter replied, but he too, was smiling.

A knock at the door silenced them. Yuko quickly gathered the *nandogami* and returned them to the closet. Only then, did Peter answer the door.

"Yuko, bring sake to our guests," Peter said, swinging wide the door. A dozen or more people entered and there was much bowing and greeting.

Once they had settled with sake cups in hand, plans began for the next day. Peter was evidently in charge.

"We will go to the Oura Cathedral. We must be very careful not to expose ourselves to the authorities or their spies," he said. All heads nodded and bowed in agreement. "But we will approach this new Bateren and learn if indeed, he is one of us."

Talk continued for over an hour. Then Yuko produced blankets and everyone made a spot to rest inside their home. Michael could not sleep until he asked Peter, "May I come too? I would like to meet the Bateren."

Peter smiled and said, "Your companionship honors us. Now sleep."

The morning came and a flurry of activity filled the little home. Peter estimated that the journey to the Nagasaki cathedral would take them a couple of hours. Though Ichiro pleaded with his father, he was not allowed to go. "You must protect your mother. You must guard the *nandogami*."

69

Ichiro was pleased with this order. He stood in a *kata* stance; much like Michael had done so long ago. "I will guard them, honorable Father!"

The journey to Nagasaki was bittersweet for Michael. He couldn't help enjoying the excitement of the others as they anticipated meeting, after 230 years, a priest to minister to them. And yet, he also remembered the last journey and the way Thomas had died.

They heard the Angelus bells ring before they saw the church and Michael knew that it was noon. It took nearly half an hour before they actually saw it. The gothic facade of the beautiful Oura Cathedral stood before them and they stared in wonder at the edifice erected for their martyrs.

"*Dozo,* please, may this be the church of our honorable God," said Peter. The others whispered, "Amen," and followed as he led them around the church. They went stealthily to the rear door, wary of being seen. Peter crossed himself and knocked on the heavy wooden door.

The door opened before them and there stood a priest. Michael saw the surprise in the man's face at the sight of Japanese people knocking on the door of a foreign church.

He sensed the hesitancy of his companions to state their business. One of the women placed her hand over her heart and knelt before the priest, saying "Tell us, is this the 17th day in the month of sorrows?"

"Lent? Yes, today is March 17th, during the time observed by Christians as a season of fasting and penitence in preparation for Easter," said the priest.

"O Deous sama, O Yaso sama, Santa Maria sama," cried the woman, "you are one of us."

"But who are you and who is your earthly leader?" Peter wanted to know. "Is he from the kingdom of Rome?"

"You mean the pope?" asked the priest. "He is the Vicar of Christ on earth, our Sovereign Pontiff,

Pius IX. And I am Fr. Bernard Petitjean, from the *Mission Etrangeres de Paris*."

Peter still seemed unsure and asked further, "Have you no children?"

"You and your Japanese brothers, both Christian and pagans, these are the children the Good Lord has given us. But we cannot have any other children, because as priests, we must, as did the first Apostles, remain celibate."

Hearing this they fell to their knees and cried, "They are virgins! *O Deous Sama*, thank you! Thank you!"

Michael, who had remained standing, saw tears roll down Fr. Petitjean's cheeks. The priest realized that Christianity had not been lost, but had been preserved in secret by the people of Japan for two and a half centuries.

Fr. Petitjean urged them to stand, "Please, do not kneel before me. Come in. Come in," Holding wide the door to the church of the martyrs, the priest stood aside as the people rose.

"His heart beats as ours," they whispered. A thought came to Michael that he'd never had before. He had always focused on the differences between himself and his father. These Japanese, who had suffered for centuries because they chose to embrace a Western religion, were weeping with joy at finding this Frenchman. Fr. Petitjean looked like any ordinary European. Much as my own father might look if he were to face these same Japanese, he thought. Only his heart beats as mine!

As they entered the church they saw a large statue of the Blessed Virgin with the Child Jesus. "The feast of *Gotanjo,* Christmas, we celebrated," Peter said and walked to the statue and bowed deeply. They stayed for nearly an hour talking to the delighted priest.

Through tears he told them, "St. Francis Xavier was right about your people. He said, 'there will not be another nation to surpass the Japanese… a people who prize honor above all else.' "

Michael liked the priest and the fact that he was not ashamed to be moved by the loyalty of the people of Japan. The resolve of his ancestors amazed him too. That they had gone into hiding and kept the flame of Christianity burning for more than two centuries was a miracle in itself.

In the days that followed Fr. Petitjean was introduced to thousands of *Kakure Krishitans.* "There are 25 Christianities in the area," Peter told him, "and seven Baptizers."

Since the ban on Christianity had not been lifted the Christians had to be discreet, but they managed to spread the word that there was a priest available.

After two days, Peter told Fr. Petitjean they must return home. He gave directions to his village and Fr. Petitjean agreed to come as soon as possible to meet the Christians there. They knelt before the priest in the Oura Cathedral and received his blessing.

When they returned to Peter's home, the village surrounded the travelers, clamoring for news of their trip. Peter told them that the Bateren would come to the village. The priests had returned to Japan!

Michael wondered if Peter was as tired as he. Later that evening, after Yuko served them a meal of rice and fish, she boiled water for tea.

Michael was not at all surprised to see three amber *chawan* with the little white crosses. He had come to expect at least one in every place he traveled. He had broken the one from Thomas, but Kosuma Takeya's sister had told him that her brother had originally made four of them. There were three left after he broke the fourth. The set from his grandmother contained two. He wondered what had happened to the other one.

Yuko scooped powdered green tea from the *natsume,* tea container, and put it into the *chawan.* Michael watched each graceful movement as she poured the hot water over the powder and gently whisked the tea. She turned the *chawan* so the front faced Michael and then handed it to him.

72

"*Goshouban sasete itadaki masu*, I will join you," Michael said. He turned the *chawan* then lifted it to his lips. He strained to keep his eyes open as he sipped the tea. Just as his legs began to tingle, his eyes started to water. Despite his efforts, he blinked. He knew that when he opened his eyes, Peter, Yuko, and the time he had spent with them would be gone.

CHAPTER EIGHT

Michael touched the floor beneath him. He felt the texture of a *tatami* mat and knew he was still lost in time. He was kneeling on a porch covered with the thick, straw mats. *Bonsai* and other potted plants stood in the garden below. A drooping cherry tree, laden with blossoms, cast its shadow over a great stone lantern in the rear of the garden. A cool breeze whispered through the tree branches and sent a shower of cherry blossoms to the ground.

A small sound behind him caught his attention. He turned to find a small man in a dark silk kimono smiling at him. The man bowed so low, Michael was afraid he might fall to the floor.

"*Irasshaimase!* Welcome to my home. I have prepared for your coming," said the man.

"My coming? How did you know I was coming?"

Instead of answering, the man said, "Michael, there is someone I would like you to meet."

Michael wondered how the man knew his name. But he was weary of all the tea traveling. He wanted only to return to his own time. Why couldn't he sip tea with one of these people and just end up at home? There had to be some reason, some element that kept him from going back, but what?

In books he had read and movies he had seen, there was usually something that had to occur. The characters in ghost stories had to help solve a mystery, or right a wrong before the ghost stopped haunting a victim.

In time travel it seemed some change had to take place before the time traveler could return home. But this wasn't a book or a movie. This was his life. And he wanted it back! Why was this happening to him? He was so full of questions.

The strange Japanese man didn't give him a chance to ask them. He spoke as if nothing was out of the ordinary, as if people typically appeared on his porch. "You honor me this night. I am Kiyoshi Takeya, tea master of Nagasaki." He gestured for Michael to follow him saying, "Come."

"I am not following you anywhere!" Michael said. "I feel like everywhere I go, everyone I meet knows what is happening to me -- except me!" The people he had seen, the tragedies they had suffered, were tearing him apart.

Kiyoshi stood calmly in front of him, expecting him to follow where he led. He did not appear in the least bit curious about Michael's increasing panic. He had not looked alarmed at all when Michael appeared out of nowhere.

Until now, it had not occurred to him that he might not ever return home. Was he going to spend the rest of his life drifting in and out of the lives of others?

He couldn't take it any longer. He didn't even try to hide his weakness or his fear. He cried in anguish at his fate. His shoulders shook and his throat grew hoarse, but he did not care. He was tired of seeing death and injustice. He was tired of failing at every turn. And he was especially tired of the spirit of the Japanese. He would never say, *Shikata ga nai,* and smile as evil men tried to destroy him.

"Tears are raindrops that wash the soul," Kiyoshi said, laying his hand on Michael's shoulder.

Michael shrugged Kiyoshi away. "You people have a saying for everything. Well, I don't care about your silly sayings. I don't care what you or anyone else thinks of me. I just want to go home."

"You are unaware that the Lord has blessed you with the bread of sorrow and the drink of tears," Kiyoshi said. "You must not lose heart because of your sadness."

"How can you know what I have been through?" Michael demanded. "I am sick of all this double talk."

"If you cannot find peace within yourself Michael, you will never bring it to another. You will be a burden to them, but more of a burden to yourself."

Michael said, "How can someone be at peace when terrible things keep happening to them? You have no idea the nightmares I have seen."

"He who knows best how to suffer will enjoy the greater peace, because he is the conqueror of himself. Peace in this miserable life is found in humbly enduring suffering; not in being free from it."

"I can't argue with you anymore; I am too tired," Michael said.

At this, Kiyoshi smiled again and said, "Then come. What other plans have you for this night?"

Michael nodded, "Okay, you win. I have no other plans."

"I am on my way to *Mugenzai no Sono,* the Garden of the Immaculata," Kiyoshi said.

"Is it far?" Michael asked, following him to the side of the house. Kiyoshi rolled out the strangest looking bicycle Michael had ever seen. Attached to the back was a buggy large enough for two people.

"It is only seven kilometers; I'll have you there before long. You ride in the *niguruma,*" he said, pointing to the buggy. It looked rather like a rickshaw secured to the end of the bike.

Michael climbed in, but felt rather foolish. He was much younger and probably stronger than Kiyoshi; he should be doing the pedaling. He mentally converted the kilometers and realized that they would travel four miles. But Kiyoshi pedaled with ease. The adjustable wooden seat had no springs under it and

76

when they unexpectedly hit a bump, Michael was sure Kiyoshi had jarred his spine. "How old is this bike anyway?" he asked.

"It is just a bit older than I, but we get on well together," said Kiyoshi.

"You said you were taking me to *Mugenzai no Sono*. Aren't we in Nagasaki?"

"We are in Nagasaki," Kiyoshi replied. "And so is the *Mugenzai no Sono*. It is a community entirely consecrated to the service of the Immaculate Virgin, whom it serves by means of printing thousands of newspapers, books and magazines." Michael learned that the Japanese mission was complete with a seminary system and a publishing house. He rode mostly in silence, watching the countryside from the *niguruma*.

"Here we are," said Kiyoshi, bringing the bicycle to a stop. He hopped off as if he hadn't just pedaled four miles.

"Some people thought Fr. Kolbe was crazy to build on Mount Hikosan. They said the steep ground sloping away from the town was unsuitable. But he is a wise priest and many others trust his judgment."

Kiyoshi's eyes danced and Michael couldn't help being amused at his excitement. He led Michael from the garden off the porch to one of several buildings in the area. The room they entered echoed with the noise of a printing press. Two men were watching the process. One, in a Franciscan robe, pulled one of the papers, hot off the press, and handed it to Michael.

"Here is a complimentary issue of, '*Seibo no Kishi*,' our 'Japanese Knight of the Immaculata,'" he said to Michael. And then to Kiyoshi, "I see you have brought another visitor."

"*Dozo*, Michael, this is our most honorable Fr. Maximilian Kolbe."

Michael caught himself. He had almost said aloud, Saint Maximilian Kolbe? Michael remembered his Catechism teacher telling them about the man who had been canonized in 1982. He also remembered that Maximilian Kolbe would be killed in Auschwitz in 1941, when he took the place of a prisoner who was about to be executed. So Michael knew he had at least made it to the twentieth century again and of course if he was meeting Fr. Kolbe, it had to be before 1941.

The frail saint took Michael's free hand and clasped it in a surprising grip saying, "Welcome to the Army of the Immaculata." He turned to Kiyoshi and said, "You nearly bring as many to our doors as we evangelize with our paper."

"It is my honor to show what the Immaculate Lady has done for us in Japan," Kiyoshi beamed. "And this," he said turning to the other man, "is Dr. Takashi Nagai. He is from the Dept. of Radiology at Nagasaki University Medical School."

"I hope you have convinced Fr. Kolbe to take some time for rest," Kiyoshi said to the doctor.

Dr. Nagai shook his head. "I tried. But you know how he is. It is clearly a miracle that he could have lived so long. His lungs are terribly lacerated from the tuberculosis."

Fr. Kolbe smiled and said, "I will have time for rest in heaven. Here, I have too much work."

"As a doctor, I advise you to rest. At the same time, I understand you are doing the work of the Lord," said Dr. Nagai.

Kiyoshi laughed, "My friends, neither of you take time for rest."

"This life is brief; like misers we must take advantage of the little time that remains to us," Fr. Kolbe spoke almost as if he anticipated how little time he had left.

Kiyoshi changed the subject abruptly, "I can expect you both this evening with Midori?" Kiyoshi asked.

Fr. Kolbe nodded and Dr. Nagai said, "Yes. Midori says to thank you for the invitation. She is honored to accept."

"Who is Midori?" Michael asked.

"Midori Moriyama is Dr. Nagai's wife. She and her family are direct descendents of the Hidden Christians. Midori's faith helped to convert Dr. Nagai," answered Kiyoshi.

"She invited me to the Mass of the rooster at Christmastime," said Dr. Nagai. "I first refused saying I was not a Christian. Midori assured me that was not important because neither were the Shepherds, or the Three Kings, but they came to worship at the stable of the Christ Child. And so I surprised myself by agreeing to accompany them. I shall never forget that midnight Mass. Five thousand Christians filled the cathedral, singing the credo in Latin. I had the *chokkan,* intuition, that there was a living 'Someone' present in the Urakami Cathedral."

"Ah, but you were still not convinced," pressed Kiyoshi.

"No, it was a difficult path. I had gone from the Shinto faith of my ancestors to atheism. But the Catholic faith magnetized me. And Midori's prayers and example led me to seek answers. I went to the cathedral of Nagasaki and spent many nights in conversation with Father Moriyama. I read the 'Thoughts' of Pascal. One crucial point I could not forget; there is light enough for those who desire to see and darkness enough for those who don't. And suddenly, everything became clear to me. I had been in darkness and I longed for the light of Christ. I was baptized in June of 1934 and took the name Paul, in honor of St. Paul Miki, our great Japanese martyr. Two months later, Midori became my wife."

Michael sensed the thread, which seemed to run from the *chawan* and the martyrs, throughout his travels. But only sensed, he could not grasp it fully.

"I look forward to seeing you this evening then," Kiyoshi said. "It has been a long time since I've seen Midori." The men shook hands and said good-bye to Kiyoshi and Michael.

Before going back to the teahouse Kiyoshi took Michael behind the monastery. There a beautiful grotto depicting Our Lady of Lourdes. "Fr. Kolbe built this grotto when he came to Nagasaki in 1931. Midori comes here often to pray for Dr. Nagai. He has leukemia." Kiyoshi said.

Michael did not tell Kiyoshi that he knew what was to happen to Fr. Kolbe. It gave him a bit of satisfaction to know that he was keeping something from him. After all, he was pretty sure that Kiyoshi knew things he wasn't telling. He remembered reading somewhere that time travelers should never tell someone what was going to happen. It could create a paradox or some problem in that person's future. He wondered if that could be why Kiyoshi was holding back information. Maybe he didn't want to create a paradox in Michael's time.

When they returned Kiyoshi said, "You may rest on the porch if you like. I have to make preparations for the tea."

Michael must have fallen asleep because the next thing he knew, Kiyoshi was gently shaking him awake. In the garden, the others were waiting. With Fr. Kolbe and Dr. Nagai was a woman in a gray satin kimono with black silk trim.

They all bowed to Michael as he came down the porch steps to greet them. Michael bowed in return. As he raised his eyes he could not help but stare at the woman. Her thick, black hair could have been spun from the same silk that lined her kimono. She was a striking woman, and Michael felt oddly connected to her. He thought of his mother when he looked at her, though they looked nothing alike.

Dr. Nagai introduced Michael and said, "This is my wife, Midori." Her handshake was gentle and Michael felt completely at ease with her.

"I hear you were given the tour of *Mugenzai no Sono* today," she said.

"I saw the printing press run the latest edition of the Japanese Knights of the Immaculata."

"Fr. Kolbe has accomplished a great deal since coming here several years ago. *Seibo no Kishi*, the Japanese Knight, has a circulation six times that of other Catholic publications in our country. His first issue ran 10,000 copies," Midori told him. She smiled and added, "Today's issue ran 65,000 copies."

"If there are other Catholic publications in Japan, why compete?" Michael wanted to know.

Fr. Kolbe answered, "It is not to compete with the other publications, but to compose a publication

80

that will spread the Virtues of Mary. Oh, how little known the Immaculate Virgin still is! When will the souls of men love the Divine Heart of Jesus with her Heart, and in the presence of His Heart love the Heavenly Father?"

Michael was a bit uncomfortable as, once again, he was reminded how little he knew his faith. He knew that Jesus was God, that Mary was His mother. But being in the presence of this saint, who lived his life spreading the faith, who would give his life to save another, Michael knew that he still was not able to make the kind of sacrifices that led Thomas and his friends to die so willingly.

Dr. Nagai said, "The world will one day know this, if you have anything to say about it, Father. You push yourself beyond capacity and still manage to do more."

"And how have you been Father Kolbe?" Midori asked.

"I have never been better. To bring within reach of all persons the happiness that comes from the presence of God is the first source of all happiness. We have been blessed that our work is to be done under the protective care of the Blessed Virgin Mary."

Midori said, "I have found the truth of these words in my own life, Father." Something glistened around her neck. It was a medal. Michael was captivated by the design. He remembered that his mother always wore around her neck a medal just like it.

Midori took the medal in her hand and held it to Michael's face. "You see it is our Lady."

Michael saw the image of Mary standing on a globe, with dazzling rays of light streaming from her outstretched hands. Framing the figure was an inscription: *Oh, Mary conceived without sin, pray for us who have recourse to thee.*

He remembered that his mother would hold him in her arms as he climbed into bed with her, and she would show him the medal and recite the prayer.

Michael remembered the sadness in her eyes; she must have known she was going to leave him.

Fr. Kolbe reached into the pocket of his robe and produced another medal like Midori's, hanging from a chain. "Here, Michael. You need Mary's protection also."

Michael took the medal and held it in the palm of his hand. He ran his fingers over the inscription and said, "My mother wore a medal like this before she died. She suffered so much. How did the medal protect her?"

Fr. Kolbe said without hesitation, "Mary is a most tender Mother, she is now, and always will be, in life and in death and in eternity. This truth can comfort us in external difficulties, but especially in those more grievous internal ones.

"That your mother suffered was painful for you. We live in a time of great penance. Let us at least know how to profit by it. Suffering is good and sweet to those who accept it willingly."

Michael said nothing. He couldn't argue with a saint! Not that he wanted to anyway. What he said made sense. It was just that Michael didn't want it to make sense. He wanted these kinds of statements to be false. They made him uneasy because they were too hard. He was too weak.

Fr. Kolbe took the medal from Michael's hands and placed it around his neck saying, "The more powerful and courageous a soul becomes with the help of God's grace, the greater the cross God places on its shoulders, so that it might mirror as closely as possible the image of the Crucified in its own life."

"Please don't tell me that greater crosses are ahead," Michael said half-joking.

"Love, which is a union of perfection, nourishes and satisfies itself solely by suffering, sacrifice and the cross."

Great, thought Michael. "I'm sorry, Father. It's not that I don't believe. It is just that I am weak. I have never been a strong person and it seems that the more sacrifice I see, the more I want nothing to do with it."

The priest traced a blessing over his head, "The bruised reed, He will not break. You may feel crippled by weakness Michael, you may be crushed with the worries of this world, but God will not condemn you for this. He will bind your wounds and heal your heart if you will let Him."

Not knowing what else to do, Michael simply said, "Thank you." He fingered the medal that hung from his neck and wondered at this new memory of his mother. Did she feel as these people did? Had she minded the suffering, or was it offered to God as some sort of sacrifice?

He had always thought his grandmother was the strongest person he had ever known. Now, he was remembering that his mother too, was strong. Was he the only one in the family who had been born weak? Why, after longing for some memory of her his entire life, did he only start remembering her as he traveled through times that were not his?

Michael wondered if these moments in the past were not moments that brushed against something in his own life. He considered that perhaps present, past, and future were not in the sequence he had always imagined. He'd seen the medal around Midori's neck and remembered something in this time, which had not happened yet, which would not happen until his own time.

He had often wondered about God and the universe in much the same way. It was all so incomprehensible if you looked at it in an orderly numbered fashion of days.

But if each moment in time was floating around in the mass that was eternity, why couldn't he connect with a moment from another time? It could happen that way he supposed. Of course that didn't explain the tea set and why the amber *chawan* seemed to be the vehicle that sent him from one time to another.

His thoughts were interrupted as Kiyoshi said, "Let us begin the evening," They all walked around the opposite side of the garden. A weathered bamboo

83

gate had been left slightly ajar, as if in welcome. Kiyoshi gave it a gentle push and it swung wide.

They walked over stepping stones wet with dew that led to a washbasin beneath a pine tree. It was obvious to Michael, watching the way Dr. Nagai looked at his wife as he placed his hand on her elbow and guided her carefully across the damp stones, that he was completely in love with her. Michael remembered what Kiyoshi had told him, and he was sorry that Midori's husband was going to die.

Kiyoshi washed at the basin, as did the others. Michael duplicated their actions. Just beyond was a small *soan*, or hut made of wood. Here, Kiyoshi left them and entered the hut alone. They sat in the garden for several moments in silence looking at the plants and appreciating the nature of their surroundings.

Then Fr. Kolbe went to the hut and entered on his knees. The others followed. Michael's eyes drank in the beauty of the simple surroundings within. The walls were unadorned and only a few carefully selected objects graced the interior. He admired the *tokonoma*, a small alcove, which held a scroll that displayed a poem written to compliment the beauty of the night.

The guests seated themselves, their legs folded beneath them. Kiyoshi entered from another room, placing in front of them small tables on which were neatly arranged dishes. "*Dozo* please, eat," Kiyoshi commanded.

Michael looked at the lacquered dishes before him. He chose a crepe made from nuts that were braised, and then baked. He bit into it and tasted not just the crepe, but also the care of the person who prepared it. In consuming the delicacy, he was recognizing the season, which prompted the growth of its ingredients. He swallowed the alien food and peace filled his soul as the crepes filled his belly. Then he sampled the broiled salmon and rice. There was little conversation as they ate the dishes before them.

When they were filled, Kiyoshi said, "I have warm *sake* to complete the meal," He poured the liquid into *sake* cups. He told them, "Drink what you will." Kiyoshi was clearing the dishes away as they finished the sake and stood. They went out to the garden again to wash. Michael followed their lead. From the garden he could see Kiyoshi inside, sweeping the already clean floor and putting fresh flowers in the tokonoma. It was all part of the Way of the Tea, this preparation to honor the guests.

Suddenly and silently Kiyoshi opened the door. Michael noticed as they again entered the room, that the scroll had been removed and replaced in the tokonoma with a bamboo basket holding a lone, white, lotus blossom and a long thin blade of grass, still wet with dew. Once they were seated again Kiyoshi said, "Do you wish to drink *cha*?"

All nodded in harmony. "Yes, thank you," Michael answered. Kiyoshi removed a caddy from a blue silken bag, sat it down, and then washed the *chawan*. There were four of them. One was the familiar amber *chawan* he had come to know. The tiny white crosses still lined the rim. The other three were white, with the lone branch of a cherry blossom circling the base and rising to the rim.

So it was somewhere between Peter and Yuko's time and this one, that the pair of *chawan* his grandmother gave to him were removed from the original set.

Kiyoshi filled a bamboo scoop with powdered green tea prepared to dump some back in the caddy, stopping in mid air, "Perhaps you would prefer to drink the tea weak, as it is very poor quality."

"No please," said Michael, "make mine stronger. I am sure it will be very good." And so Kiyoshi dumped the powdered tea into the amber *chawan,* poured hot water into the cup, whisked it with a cane brush and placed it in front of Michael.

"You drink first," Kiyoshi said to Michael.

"No, you first," Michael told him. This was all part of the ceremony. In humbling himself as Kiyoshi did, when he said the tea was poor quality,

Michael was supposed to humble himself by taking a position behind the other.

"You are my guest. I insist," Kiyoshi said.

Michael wrapped his fingers around the *chawan* and slowly sipped the tea. His legs began to tingle just as he closed his eyes.

CHAPTER NINE

Michael opened his eyes. He was still in Nagasaki, still in Kiyoshi's home. The same cherry tree stood in the center of the garden, the same iron lantern stood in the rear. But some things were different. The blossoms that had previously burdened the tree were gone. The cool spring breeze that had played in the branches as he'd walked with Kiyoshi was silent. The air was a sticky blanket. It was dark and hot. Sweat trickled down his back as he stood.

He saw in the darkness the whisper of a man. It was Kiyoshi kneeling in the garden. Michael called out to him, "Kiyoshi, I am still here." The old man crossed himself with the crucifix at the end of his rosary, kissed it, and stood.

"Yes. You are still here."

"But time has passed?"

"Yes, time has surely passed," Kiyoshi still radiated confidence, but the lines in his face were deeper and Michael read them as worry. His hands were older than his face. He continued to finger the rosary beads, rubbing them one by one between his thumb and forefinger. The motion spoke of prayer and the nature of it in Kiyoshi's life.

Crickets chirped loudly in the darkness. Michael remembered his dad telling him, that the warmer the night, the faster they chirp.

"The early hour is to be esteemed, is it not? Not quite morning, yet no longer the night, it is a gentle yawning into day." The calmness of the Kiyoshi's words fell on his shoulders like a fine silk kimono; but Michael still had a sense of foreboding.

"Are you what is keeping me here, Kiyoshi?" he asked. "You do know how I got here don't you?" Kiyoshi placed his hand on Michael's shoulder.

"Peace comes from within Michael. But it is often nourished with the nature of one's surroundings. Come, there are certain things you must know." Kiyoshi walked ahead, and Michael followed.

A massive structure grew larger as they approached. "This is Urakami Cathedral. The largest and finest Cathedral in the Orient, it took 30 years to complete." Kiyoshi told him.

The beautiful stone building was impressive. Two large bell towers topped the steeples of red brick that rose to meet the sky. At their base, statues of St. John the Evangelist and the Virgin Mary stood; sentinels at the entrance. Michael couldn't imagine something taking 30 years to build.

As if reading his thoughts Kiyoshi added, "Thirty years is a small drop in the stream of faith that runs through Nagasaki. We stand in the Catholic heart of Japan. Tens of thousands of Japanese Christians died here. Holy Martyrs Hill, where the first 26 martyrs were crucified, is not far. Arrested in Kyoto and Osaka, they were forced to walk through the snow over 300 miles to Nagasaki. Their left ears were cut off and with blood flowing from their wounds; they were led through the villages to terrorize other Christians.

"They remained on their crosses for weeks. Christians collected their bloodied garments and miracles were attributed to the relics. We have them still here in our Cathedral." This last bit of information was new to Michael.

He listened to Kiyoshi as he explained, "Japan martyred more Christians than the Roman Empire, many right here. The Nagasaki earth has been saturated with the blood of her saints." Kiyoshi held the heavy door open for Michael to enter. Hundreds of candles lit by the Japanese faithful brightened the interior of the church. The scent of incense tickled his nostrils and spirits of the martyrs filled the air. Michael remembered Dr. Nagai's *chokkan*, his intuition of a Presence. Michael experienced that *chokkan* now. It was as if Thomas and the others stood around him in this sacred place, but it was more even than the communion of saints. For Michael knew and felt the Presence of God, there on the altar, behind the tabernacle doors.

Michael followed Kiyoshi up the narrow aisle of the cathedral and both of them bowed low before the altar. They walked through the sacristy into another area of the church. The room was filled with objects of faith.

"These objects were sheltered for centuries despite the danger it posed to Christians," Kiyoshi said proudly. He pointed to a *nandogami*. It was a statue of Buddha with a crucifix cleverly hidden in the hollow of the statue. There were gold and brass reliquaries that held bits of bloodied cloth and bone.

Remembering Peter and Yuko's joy when they learned the priests had returned to Japan, Michael asked, "But after Father Petitjean discovered the Hidden Christians in 1865, they didn't have to hide any longer, did they? That was the end of the persecutions right?"

Kiyoshi shook his head, "Like maple leaves torn from the tree in a mountain wind, the Christians of Japan were torn from Urakami. Thousands of Urakami Christians were exiled. Some were jailed and suffered such harsh conditions many died."

"It's hard to believe they didn't just give up their faith," Michael said.

"Not only did they not give up their faith Michael, but they held on to their *seishinseii*, their whole hearted devotion, to Christ and the Virgin Mother, despite hundreds of years persecution and torment. When faced with the choice of apostasy or exile the greater number courageously stood loyal to their faith."

"How can a country destroy its own people that way? It doesn't make sense. Why didn't somebody stop them?" He would never understand the cruelty of those deaths.

Kiyoshi paused as if searching for an answer that would, if not satisfy, at least explain. "One cannot grow reason in the garden of myth," he finally said.

"You see, most ancient Japanese believed the emperor was directly descended from the gods. And so, they thought they were superior to other nations. In 1638 Iemitsu, with the blood not yet dry from the massacre of the Shimabara Christians sent an edict saying, 'So long as the Sun shall warm the earth, let no Christian dare to come to Japan'. The door of Japan, like a giant snapping turtle, clamped shut her jaws. For nearly 230 years Christians went into hiding."

Kiyoshi removed a set of keys from the pocket of his kimono and opened the first display case. He removed a cloth-covered board, with a thin sheet of rice paper mounted in the center. Kiyoshi said, "This has been preserved from the early martyrs." He handed the board to Michael and said, "It is a letter from St. Thomas Kozaki. He was about your age, when he wrote his last words to his *okasan*, his mother."

Shivering, Michael took the board reverently in his hands. He remembered Thomas asking him to deliver the letter, and Thomas' father taking the letter before the guards could see it. The thin rice paper was filled with the characters Thomas had written centuries before.

Standing next to him, Kiyoshi read in a clear voice what Thomas had written:

"Dearest Mother, I am writing to you by the Grace of God. So far there are twenty-four of us…"

"But there were twenty-six!" Michael interrupted.

"Yes, two more were captured after this letter was written," Kiyoshi said. He continued, "We are

90

heading to Nagasaki to be crucified. We have been marched through the streets of each town and our sentence is displayed on a board in front of us.

"Please do not worry about *Otosan,* Father and me. We hope to see you very soon, there in paradise. Please give my love to my brothers, and keep them from the hands of the unbelievers. You and they too, shall come to an end one day. I pray that you will not lose the happiness of heaven. I commend you to Our Lord, and I send you my prayers.

"I love you always my dear *Okasan.* Until we meet again. With love, your son, Thomas."

At the bottom of the page it said, "Signed this second day of the Twelfth Moon, in Mihara fortress, in the kingdom of Aki."

"So his letter reached her then?" Michael asked.

"It was removed from the sleeve of his father's kimono. A sympathetic guard passed it on to her once the bodies were removed," Kiyoshi took the board and placed it back in the case, locking the door.

Michael made his way around the other displays. He stopped abruptly to stare at the contents in the second case.

The amber bits of a broken *chawan* were displayed on a pale blue square of satin. He could still see the bloodstains that had soaked through the fabric; they had turned brown through the years. The old woman, Kosuma Takeya's sister, had saved the broken *chawan*! Why? Michael wondered. Had she known its value?

Wait a minute! Kiyoshi said his family name was Takeya, and he owned one of the four *chawan*. He too, must be a descendent of the sword maker. He too, was Michael's ancestor.

Closing the door to the reliquary, Kiyoshi said, "I am blessed to live so near to the Cathedral. It is my sanctuary in times of trouble. I've never come before the Divine Master, hidden in the Tabernacle, without being strengthened for all that lies ahead."

But Michael was only half listening as they left the church. He was still considering the blood of the sword maker, and the generations of persecuted Christians that followed him. Their blood runs through my veins, Michael thought. He wondered if he should voice the question he longed to ask? Perhaps if Kiyoshi knew who he was he would be willing to tell him the secrets he knew. Michael decided to drop a name and see if it sparked any interest.

"Kiyoshi, you wouldn't happen to know someone named Beth - I mean, Elizabeth Endo, would you?"

A smile struggled across his face, "Yes my sister married one of the Endo family. His name is, Shiro. They have a granddaughter, Elizabeth. They live in America," The last sentence robbed him of his smile and sadness settled in his eyes. "This war has separated families. I can only hope they are well."

Michael couldn't concern himself with paradoxes now. It was all too complicated. He was in a paradox anyway wasn't he? After all, how could he be here, when he wasn't even born yet?

"Kiyoshi, what do you think about time travel?"

Kiyoshi thought for a moment and then said, "Have you heard the expression *chazen ichimi?*"

"No," Michael replied.

"It is an expression often used by tea masters. It means that the taste of tea and the taste of Zen are the same. They both absorb the wind in the pines. It is the present moment that is to be savored, Michael, with no longing for more. To find magnificence in the very essence of what is given to us in that moment."

"But Kiyoshi," Michael protested, "If I'm not supposed to be concerned with past or future and only aware of the present - then why have I come here through the tea? Why am I here in the past? Because I am you know! You do know, don't you?"

The old man gazed silently at him for several moments. Michael could hear the wind in the pines singing softly. Kiyoshi's wise old eyes spoke even before he did. "Ah, and just where are you?"

"I am here, with you in the past," Michael answered.

"Yes, you are here, with me. But I am not in the past, so how can you be? You are here with me in my present moment. Is this not the present for you also?" Michael felt a seed of understanding float softly somewhere in his mind. But it was out of his grasp.

"I wish I could figure this out. I was here in the spring, when the cherry blossoms were full. I closed my eyes and when I opened them the blossoms were gone and it was hot."

"Yes," agreed Kiyoshi, "we have entered the *mushimushi*, hot and humid days of *Hachigatsu*, August," Kiyoshi answered.

"What day is it, Kiyoshi?" Michael asked the question outright. "And what year?"

"It is the ninth day of *Hachigatsu* in the year of 1945," Kiyoshi said.

It only took a moment for Michael to realize the significance of that date. Except for the internment camps, the atrocities suffered by the Japanese were unknown to Michael before he had witnessed them in his travels. Not this time. This time he knew.

Dear God, help me, he thought. On August 9th, 1945 an atomic bomb exploded over Nagasaki, reducing it to a wasteland.

He couldn't remember the exact time it would explode. But it would explode. Would he still be here then? Would he be protected if he were? Can a person be killed in a time in which they are not yet born? His heart ached with the uncertainties. He looked at Kiyoshi and wondered too, if he would live through the day.

The last of the evening fireflies had retired with the evening sky. The chirping crickets had gone to sleep. A few people had started to spill into the street. Day was no longer yawning. It had awakened. The gentle sound of water flowing over rocks in the distance disturbed rather than relaxed his mind. A heavy sadness crushed his chest; this world was about

93

to be destroyed. He was consumed with the pending loss. He knew that a centuries old way of life was nearing an end. And he might very well be caught in the middle of the destruction. He was a butterfly caught in the spider's web.

Michael felt sick. He continued walking with Kiyoshi, but he was having trouble fighting the fear that rose in his throat. He was still a weakling. He would never change.

Kiyoshi said, "Fr. Nishida and his assistant, Fr. Tamaya, are hearing confessions this morning. I must keep the midnight fast before receiving the Sacrament. You are welcome to join me for the Sacrament or I can provide you with a bite to eat now."

Yes, thought Michael. I could talk to the priest. They hear all sorts of things in confession. Besides if he thinks I'm crazy he won't be able to come out and tell everyone else. He wouldn't try to have me put away or anything. The seal of confession was sacred!

"I'll keep the fast and go to Church with you," Michael said. He vaguely remembered learning that the Communion fast long ago was from midnight the night before.

If only he knew what time the bomb would hit. He wanted to warn Kiyoshi, at least they should hide, and they should do something to protect themselves. He seemed to remember that those who were wearing white, where protected from the worst rays.

Oh, why hadn't he paid more attention to such things! He knew the date had been engraved in the heart of history. He just couldn't remember the time.

A screaming siren shattered the morning stillness and Michael, fell to his knees, covered his ears and trembled. Kiyoshi put his hands under Michael's elbow and pulled him to his feet.

"Do not worry. It is just another air raid. Michael shrugged his support away. "I'm fine now," he said. He hasn't got a clue what I'm really scared of, thought Michael. He had been sure the bomb was above him. But the screaming stopped as suddenly as it had started.

A different alarm sounded and Kiyoshi assured Michael quickly, "It is the all clear signal. We are safe."

No, we're not, thought Michael. No, we're not!

Back in Kiyoshi's little kitchen, Michael tried to help prepare for their meal after Mass. Kiyoshi handed Michael a thick pot with a heavy lid for him to sit aside. Then Kiyoshi poured water from a large pitcher into a large bowl half-filled with rice. "We will have toasted tea poured over rice," he said.

Michael was still wondering how to warn Kiyoshi. If he announced his fears Kiyoshi would think he was crazy. Even if Kiyoshi believed him, he would not know what to do. Michael knew that the destruction took place in the morning. It was morning now. How far could they get on Kiyoshi's ancient bicycle?

And then it was time to go to the Urakami Cathedral. They walked out into the sunlight. Michael looked at the trees and the beauty of the Urakami valley and felt tears well up inside him. He closed his eyes, clenched his fists and willed himself strong. What a pathetic joke I am, he thought. How much time is left? Think, he exclaimed in his mind. But the more he tried to make himself think the harder it was to do so. What should he do? Should he tell Kiyoshi they should change into white clothing? Or run to the shelter?

Once again, they walked up to the doors of the cathedral. This time, Michael opened the door for Kiyoshi. Surely they would be more protected inside this huge building.

The countless candles still flickered, the smell of incense, still hung in the air. But this time the church was not empty. Michael had never seen a church filled this way for confession! White lace covered the heads of women and girls, who knelt on the epistle side of the church.

Michael genuflected with Kiyoshi and knelt beside him with the other men on the Gospel side. He watched as two Japanese priests bowed before the altar and then walked down the aisle. He turned his head to see which priest went into each confessional. A purple stole hung across the center door of each. They each picked up their stole, kissed it, placed it around their neck, entered the confessional and closed the door behind them.

Michael's heart pounded in anticipation. He waited until Kiyoshi finished with his examination of conscience and stood to enter the confession line.

Michael went over what he was going to say to the priest. I ought to confess my sins too, he thought. It was something he'd never really taken seriously till now. He decided he would confess his sins, especially those that concerned his resentment of his father and his terribly weak spirit. Then he would tell about the bomb. Maybe the priest would help him to tell people. Maybe they could save some of them.

The line moved as one by one, each Christian knelt before the priest. And then Kiyoshi tapped Michael on the shoulder to let him know he was entering the confessional and Michael was next. He turned from the altar and faced the confessional as the others had done at this point. He watched as Kiyoshi made his way…

And then a blinding light flashed inside the Cathedral. It was as if a great clap of lightening had ripped open the Cathedral dome, shedding an awful brightness. Michael looked up and saw that the roof was gone, an enormous cloud swelled upward into a great column of smoke. He saw the windows shatter and a great gust of wind threw glass shards like leaves in autumn.

The shards slashed Kiyoshi's body and the wind slammed him like a little doll into the brick wall. And then the wall and Kiyoshi were simply gone, hurled into the Nagasaki landscape. That landscape, moments before so beautiful, was terrifying.

Houses and people were uprooted and cast into the atmosphere. When they fell to the ground they were smashed to pieces. Clumps of trees vanished, as the force of destruction wiped out everything in its path as it rapidly made its way across the valley. Only Michael stood fixed where he was. He watched in horror as life was erased before his eyes.

And then blackness was everywhere. Michael wondered if he had gone blind from terror. He rubbed his eyes with trembling hands. He opened them again, seeing only darkness. He thought he was alone in that world until he heard a cry, "*Tasukete!* Help!" Michael walked in the direction of the voice. He still couldn't see anything. He stumbled over something. He bent down and touched it. An arm, or perhaps a leg, it was soft and wet. It was severed from its body and Michael was glad that it was too dark to see. He ran in the darkness, but he knew as he did so that he had nowhere to run.

Then darkness gave way to an eerie redness. Fires had broken out around him. Flames licked at the bodies of those who had died, some on their knees, others with arms raised upward as if reaching for something.

Michael gave an anguished cry that would not end. He fell to his knees in the Nagasaki ash and felt the stinging hot flames that ran across the bodies nearby. He had no strength. He lay down, near the dead and dying and wished it would end. He did not want his strength to return. He embraced the despair that made him weak and hoped that he too, would die. As his mind shut down, cries swirled around him, "*Mizu!* Water!" He heard the torment as others pleaded too. Michael had been untouched by the blast, and was not afflicted with their terrible thirst. But all those living around him were not so lucky. When he closed his eyes, tears slipped from them and ran down his cheeks.

Rain fell from the sky and woke him. Michael didn't know if he'd been unconscious or just asleep. He looked down and saw that he was covered with a greasy black film. He remembered something about 'black rain' and radioactive debris.

He couldn't stay here any longer. He stood. It did not matter which direction he walked, he vowed to walk until he dropped or found help, whichever came first. He saw bodies naked, bloated, skinless, some still alive, still begging, *"Mizu!"*

Their clothes had been burned or ripped from their bodies, their skin peeled away from their limbs hanging by shreds as they lumbered about in agony. He knew they could not live long. After walking about an hour, the black rain finally stopped falling on the valley. When it stopped, so did Michael. He felt as if he were made of lead, and yet he was dizzy. A paradox he thought, and laughed in a crazy way that made him think he was demented.

There were others groaning about him also. He had made it to the side of a hill where survivors had gathered. He saw a man giving directions to some others as they cared for some of the wounded. The man had a bandage around his head. He knew him. Michael found strength in the sight of someone familiar and ran towards him.

"Dr. Nagai," he screamed. Dr. Nagai turned and recognized Michael.

"You have not been hurt?" the doctor asked.

"No. I am fine," said Michael. "But Kiyoshi…" Michael sobbed, "is dead."

Dr. Nagai shook his head. It was one more friend that he had lost. Michael realized that this man probably knew many of the dead and suffering. "I must go now to find my wife; I have done all I can here."

Michael nodded and then watched as Dr. Nagai walked away from him back into the village. Michael followed him. Though the village had been annihilated Dr. Nagai made his way towards his home with determination. When he stopped before a pile of rubble and ash, Michael knew that it had been the doctor's home.

In a pile of ash and bone, the doctor found his wife. Michael recalled how he had gently helped Midori over the stones in Kiyoshi's garden. Just as tenderly he now gathered her bones, placing them in a pail found in the ruins. In the bones of her right hand the doctor found the melted chain and cross of her rosary.

He bowed his head, "My God, I thank you for permitting her to die while she prayed. Mary, Mother of sorrows, thank you for having been with her at the hour of her death… Jesus, You carried the heavy cross until you were crucified upon it. Now, you come to shed the light of peace on the mystery of suffering and death, Midori's and mine…"

Then he looked at Michael and concluded, "Fate is strange. I believed so strongly that it would be Midori that would carry me to the tomb… Now her poor remains are resting in my arms… Her voice seems to murmur: forgive, forgive."

He stood cradling the pail with his wife's remains; he walked from the ruins of his home and into the ruins of his homeland, Nagasaki. Michael followed him in silence.

And then he saw it, but only a remnant of its former glory. The scarred southern corner of the sanctuary and its jagged remains were all that was left of the great Urakami Cathedral. He thought of looking for Kiyoshi's ashes, to give him a decent burial, as Dr. Nagai had done for Midori. But he knew that it was futile. The cathedral had many people inside when the bomb exploded. Michael knew that any remains had been incinerated when the fires broke out.

Where the great Urakami Cathedral had once stood, only the scarred, blasted southern wall of the sanctuary of its façade remained. The sorrowful virgin had remained standing, chipped and scorched from the blast.

Michael would never forget the sights he had witnessed. The statue of the Sorrowful Mother would forever be a part of that memory.

CHAPTER TEN

Around midnight, Michael heard women's voices, singing Latin Hymns. He was too exhausted to think much about it but he passed a place the next morning and found the badly burned bodies of twenty-seven nuns from the Josei convent. He knew then that it was their voices singing those hymns the night before.

The explosion had demolished the convent and killed some of the nuns instantly. But Dr. Nagai said the twenty-seven that were horribly burned, clustered around that little stream, had obviously died in agony. Yet they had died singing those hymns. Suffering, they managed to lift their voices and their hearts to heaven!

The same was true of the girls from Junshin School, where Midori had once taught. Dr. Nagai had visited a sick elderly woman, who was dying with radiation disease. Michael heard her say, "Your Midori would have been so proud. She taught them well."

"Yes," the doctor agreed. "As the air raids intensified, the principal, Sr. Ezumi, had the whole school sing a hymn every day for God's protection. The opening line was, 'Mary, Mother! I offer myself to you, body, soul and spirit.'"

The woman nodded her head in agreement. "Yes Dr. Nagai, the morning of the mushroom cloud the girls were scattered in many different places. But wherever groups of them were together, even though they would be dead within a few days, they were heard singing the song Sr. Ezumi had taught them, 'Mother Mary I offer myself to you.'"

Michael wasn't sure how many days had passed since the bombing. Time dissolved into an occasion of shock that never ended. Days and nights ran together just as Midori's rosary beads had melted into the chain that had once connected them.

Michael didn't stop to wonder why he had been untouched by the blast, the radiation, and the fires. Not then. Not at that time. He roamed around, stunned. Nothing he had ever learned about the bombing could have prepared him for this ghastly view of man's inhumanity to man.

He tried to stay close to Dr. Nagai. Sometimes without saying anything he would just follow him. Michael wasn't spying. But there was a small comfort, in that unknown and tragic world, to find someone recognizable, and to find him or her alive. Michael wasn't going to lose him.

The horrors he had witnessed had anesthetized him so that he hardly touched his worry of going home. There wasn't time to consider his own needs, when so many around him were suffering. So he left that anxiety deep in his mind. Finding the amber *chawan* and returning home were simply not important in the world in which he found himself.

There were only a couple of instances when his anxiety nearly surfaced, but then he would encounter a survivor so wretched that even Michael, who had been weak all his life, could not turn from their pain to think of his own. And there was little time left to think anyway.

He accompanied Dr. Nagai to Koba, where his son, ten-year-old Makoto and his daughter, three-year-old Kayano, waited with their *obaason* for the return of their parents. Only Dr. Nagai was left to them, and he would not last long. Michael knew the pain of losing his mother, but these children were going to lose their father as well.

Michael did not go inside the little house at first. He didn't want to intrude on the family at such a personal time. Most of the survivors had been robbed of their private grief. They could not go inside their homes, shut the door on the world and mourn. Their raw anguish was as open to the world as their wounds. The bomb had ripped and burned the clothes from their bodies, cremated their homes and families, and revealed each intimate tragedy in all its gruesome details.

Michael wandered from one group of survivors to another. They would rarely bother to identify themselves. They would simply appear and work side by side. But he always managed to remain as close as possible to Dr. Nagai.

Even finding survivors was a test in fortitude. While one would normally find solace in the fact there were any survivors at all, the state of many of these survivors was horrifying. Patients could have hundreds of different wounds. Some of the wounds were cuts they received from flying debris, with bits of concrete, glass, and wood still embedded in what flesh remained on their bodies. Some people had so many splinters they were like pincushions. Added to this were pitiful burns. As they lay suffering, waiting for rescue and treatment, wounds became infected. Once located, these patients were so gruesome and swollen they looked monstrous. One by one they were dying a grotesque and painful death.

The "three mountain" region of Mitsuyama was chosen as the site for a first aid station. The mineral springs flowing behind the range were known for their healing properties.

Michael spent his time volunteering in the first aid station, and then helping clear away the rubble and the dead in the Urakami valley. He noticed through it all that Dr. Nagai remained dedicated. He had a way of looking at the revolting and finding good in it. Michael remembered what Thomas had said about *wabi* and finding beauty in the unadorned. But Nagasaki was not just unadorned. It was scourged by the enemy, and decomposing before their eyes.

While he was throwing wood on a funeral pyre with another volunteer he asked, "How can Dr. Nagai find beauty in any of this?"

102

"It is not in the destruction," the other man told him. "It is in the spirit of those who were destroyed. You are looking only at the suffering bodies, the violated earth. You must look at what grows from the earth. You must see beyond the tortured bodies."

It was more of that mysterious talk that Michael did not understand. "How can people find peace in such surroundings?" he demanded.

"The people alone and of themselves cannot." The man answered. "It is only through Christ, and with Mary, our Morning Star, that peace among these ruins can be found. Can we see a lily in the field of death? Where is the purpose of life, but in death and what comes after?"

Michael tried hard to understand. He wished that he could accept such a philosophy. They finished stacking the wood and stood back as two other men piled first one mutilated body, and then another atop the pyre. When the men could no longer reach the top, they sprayed the bodies with oil to prepare the pyre for the mass cremation.

Michael joined some of the other men for a brief rest. They sat at the foot of a tree, standing naked from the blast. A pretty young woman, wearing the typical trousers worn by most Japanese women, approached them. Her hair was pulled back and hung, long, down her back. She carried a large basket. She reached in and drew out roasted sweet potatoes and passed them around to the men. At first they nibbled without thought, and then one of the men looked around and must have remembered that he wasn't really very hungry after all.

She looked at him sadly and said, "I know, it is hard to think of our own bellies at this time. But your efforts are needed. You cannot continue without nourishment."

The man looked at her, then at the potato. Michael thought for a moment he was going to throw it to the ground. Instead he nodded, his Adam's apple moved slowly, and then he swallowed. Michael forced down the lump in his own throat.

And then she stood in front of him. She smiled and handed him a potato. He took it, and to please her, bit into it. He had never liked sweet potatoes. But that didn't matter since he couldn't taste it anyway.

Something about the woman was familiar. Or was it just that she was uninjured like him? Perhaps she had come from another city to volunteer. Then he heard a burst of air as the funeral pyre was ignited and erupted into flames. He looked out across the valley at other fires like this one and he shuddered.

He didn't want to take another bite. People were dead and dying all around him and he was trying to decide how he could eat a stupid potato, or get rid of it without her knowing that he had done so.

She looked at him and said, "*Tabete kudasai*. Please eat."

But Michael could not. The woman seemed about to say something else, but she hesitated. She looked at Michael and he sensed her sadness. She shifted the basket of sweet potatoes from one arm to the other. "Walk with me for a while?" she asked.

Michael looked to the others, and the man he'd been working with said, "Go ahead. You've been at it a long time." And so Michael stood and went with the woman. They walked over the blackened landscape, past the injured, past the dead. They passed a set of stone steps that had been blown from a building and Michael saw the imprint of a human shadow stamped forever on the granite. He trembled, thinking of the person who had been incinerated, leaving only an outline on the step.

"I hate the Americans for having done this," Michael said.

"Don't." Michael stared at her. How could she say that?

"Some in the Japanese Imperial Army have committed their own crimes. The horrifying deaths of innocent people have bloodied their hands also. The prisoners of war in the Bataan Death March were killed mercilessly, and those who survived suffered very much. Many in the Imperial Army even took pleasure in brutally massacring our Asian brothers in Nanking."

"How do you know all this?" Michael wanted to know. Little news had filtered to the cities of Japan during the war, and certainly it was not reported as she said.

"I speak the truth. War is a terrible thing. Scripture says swords should be beaten into plowshares, and spears into pruning hooks. It says that nation shall not lift up sword against nation, neither shall they learn war any more." Her last words were so soft he could barely hear them.

After walking for a while in silence Michael said, "Where are we going?"

"There is something I want you to see," she answered. He didn't press her about their destination. He was content to walk with someone who had been untouched by the blast. He was tired of seeing pain. He was even more tired of feeling guilty for remaining whole.

And then, they were no longer in the blackened ruins. The smell of death and decay faded as they entered *Mugenzai no Sono,* The Garden of the Immaculate. Kiyoshi's words came back to Michael, "Some people thought Fr. Kolbe was crazy to build on Mount Hikosan. They said the steep ground sloping away from the town was unsuitable. But he is a wise priest and many others trust his judgment."

Michael stared at the area and at the buildings Fr. Kolbe had built. It had suffered only minor damage. The only damage appeared to be a few broken panes from the stained glass windows.

"Fr. Kolbe's choice of location was providential don't you think?" the woman asked. Michael nodded. The hills had protected the Garden of the Immaculate. St. Maximilian Kolbe's, *Mugenzai no Sono* still stood.

Michael went with her to the Lourdes Grotto. It was here that Midori had carried prayers for Dr. Nagai. The woman knelt in the grotto and Michael got down on his knees beside her. He poured his heart out to Mary, and begged her to intercede for him to her Son.

Michael thought he had said more prayers since traveling in time, than he had in his entire life. They stood and left the grotto and walked back the way they had come.

When they entered the thickness of the destruction Michael was glad that he had been given a chance to get away from it for a while. The woman must have realized that the sights plagued him. They stood again, near the men Michael had been working with. How quickly they had walked to the grotto and returned.

Michael studied the woman. She had tears in her eyes. Looking intently at him, she raised her hand, placed it on his head and swept back a strand of hair.

Instead of being shocked at her boldness Michael felt his insides go weak. He wanted to hug this woman. He wondered why she seemed so familiar. He had followed her, and for the first time since he'd found him, he'd lost sight of Dr. Nagai. He hadn't even questioned where they were going. His mouth felt dry and he remembered the words of all those people as they cried for *mizu,* water.

"Who are you?" Michael wanted to know. Her eyes darted about as if the answer would be found in the air. But it was not found, or she chose not to give it.

"Always remember, Michael, it is only love through the Sacred Heart of Christ that can truly win souls. And the hatred of war can so easily damn them," she said. Then she slowly let her hand slip from his head. When her fingers left his brow the emotion that had filled his heart evaporated. He closed his eyes against the sting that threatened to surface.

Like Kiyoshi, this woman knew something, he was sure of it. He opened his eyes to look at her. She was gone. She had walked away from him. He could still see her as she walked away in the distance. "Wait," he called to her. "Come back. Please…"

106

She heard him. He knew she did. But she did not answer. She kept walking, her back straight and purposeful. Michael did not chase her. What was the use? Then he remembered something. The woman had called him Michael. But he had not told her his name. He scanned the black horizon in search of her. She was gone. He couldn't even tell which direction she had actually been going; the land around him was blackened devastation on all sides. He started running in the direction he thought it might have been. He ran until his side hurt.

Instead of finding the woman he found Dr. Nagai. He was treating a young girl whose gums were bleeding. She had lost patches of hair and her scalp was showing through. Michael had seen others like her. Many who thought they'd been saved because they were spared injuries from flying debris and fire learned quickly that they had been damaged on the inside by radiation.

A young medical student came running towards them. "Listen," he cried. He carried a small radio and he sat it on the box of medical supplies. "All of Japan has been ordered to stand by for an announcement." He fiddled with the dials, trying to rid the little box of static in the airwaves.

A young nurse, who had been helping the doctor asked, "Is the Imperial Army going to ask us to repel the American enemy as our ancestors repelled the Mongols in the thirteenth century?"

"Are any of us up to such a task?" the student asked. And then the crackling static was replaced by a voice over the radio. They were stunned into silence as Emperor Hirohito broke the imperial silence and spoke publicly for the first time.

The Emperor spoke in a high-pitched voice, "The time has come," he said, for "Enduring the unendurable and suffering what is insufferable." The war was over. Japan had surrendered. Michael knew all of this but now he witnessed it in the anguish of those around him. Dr. Nagai and the others fell to their knees in grief facing towards the Emperor, their foreheads on the ground.

107

Michael went over to Dr. Nagai and gently laid his hand on the man's shoulder. "But this is good," he reasoned. "The war is over."

Dr. Nagai raised his eyes to Michael and said, "Our Japan, symbolized by Mt. Fuji rising up through the clouds, the first mountain to be touched by the rays of the sun when it rises in the East, our Japan is dead!"

Michael wondered if Dr. Nagai had finally reached his breaking point. But his melancholy did not last. He rallied quickly and urged those around him to do so also.

Everyone sought the doctor's advice. They would come to him when the last patient had been cared for, and they would stay for hours into the night. The conversation always carried reports of certain people that were killed and what they were doing as they breathed their last. Dr. Nagai listened intently to each.

Later that day, Michael saw Dr. Nagai sitting on a pile of rubble inside the broken cathedral. Michael had heard that the Bishop had invited the doctor to speak to the people of Nagasaki on the day of the open-air Mass that would be offered for the dead.

Michael supposed the doctor was thinking of what he would say in his speech at the open air Mass. In the fading light, charred timbers lying crisscross took on the appearance of the black limbs of plum trees in winter. "Black," the doctor muttered, "like the rain and the sun on August 9 and like the sun in the book of Revelation."

He gazed at the broken altar… "The Lamb that was slain! The Lamb of Revelation was followed wherever he went by a "white robed choir of virgins singing." Dr. Nagai gripped his pencil and wrote his thoughts. Michael could hear him speaking softly as he wrote, "The twenty-seven Josei nuns and the girls from Junshin School had died singing the new song learned from the Lamb. It was the song of the redemptive dimension of suffering and death. The holocaust of Calvary gave meaning and beauty to the

108

holocaust of Nagasaki." Michael sat just a short distance away listening to the beauty of the man's thoughts. He heard him as he poured his soul onto the paper.

"Maidens like white lilies
Consumed in the burning flames
As a whole burnt sacrifice
And they were singing."

The day of the Requiem Mass the Nagasaki Catholics gathered beside the ruins of their beloved cathedral. It had taken their ancestors thirty years to build the cathedral, Kiyoshi had proudly told him. Those who had built it had survived three centuries of persecution. On August 9, Michael's own Christian country had reduced the greatest cathedral in the Orient to ash, and incinerated the faithful people inside.

The crowd watched as Dr. Nagai rose and bowed to the priests, and then to them. He said to them, "At 11:02 a.m., an atom bomb exploded over our suburb. In an instant, 8,500 Catholics were called to God, and in a few hours flames turned to ash this venerable Far Eastern holy place. At midnight that night the remains of our cathedral burst into flames and were consumed. At exactly that same time in the Imperial Palace, His Majesty the Emperor made known his decision to end the war. On August 15, the Imperial Decree which put an end to the fighting was formally promulgated and the whole world saw the light of peace."

The doctor paused for a moment and then continued, "August 15 is also the date that St. Francis Xavier, our first Christian preacher arrived in Japan. August 15 is also the great feast of the Assumption of the Virgin Mary. It is significant, I believe, that Urakami Cathedral was dedicated to her. We must ask, "Were these events, the end of the war and the celebration of her feast day, merely coincidental or was it the mysterious Providence of God?

"Is there not a profound relationship between the annihilation of Nagasaki and the end of the war? Was not Nagasaki the chosen victim, the lamb without blemish, slain as a whole-burnt offering on an altar of sacrifice, atoning for the sins of all nations during World War II? "We are the inheritors of Adam's sin...of Cain's sin. He killed his brother. Yes, we have forgotten we are God's children. We have turned to idols and forgotten love. Hating one another, killing one another, joyfully killing one another! At last the evil and horrific conflict came to an end, but mere repentance was not enough for peace. We had to offer a stupendous sacrifice. Cities had been leveled but even that was not enough. Only this offering of Nagasaki sufficed and at that same moment God inspired the Emperor to issue the sacred proclamation that ended the war. The Christian flock of Nagasaki has been true to the faith through three centuries of persecution. During the recent war it prayed ceaselessly for a lasting peace. Here was the one pure lamb that had to be sacrificed on His altar. Wasn't Nagasaki the chosen victim, the spotless lamb, the holocaust offered upon the altar of sacrifice, killed for the sins of all the nations during the Second World War?"

But Michael gasped along with many in the crowd when Dr. Nagai said, "Let us be thankful that Nagasaki has been chosen for this holocaust. Let us be thankful, for through this sacrifice, peace has been given to the world as well as religious freedom to Japan."

The human part of Michael rebelled at such talk. How could he be thankful, or expect these people to be thankful that they had been maimed, their homes destroyed and their families killed? And then he remembered Thomas and the others who had all died singing. The spirit of God was in them. Is that where the strength came from, he wondered?

As the doctor spoke, his words like spiritual food were digested into the souls of those around

110

him. Michael noticed angry fists gently unfurl, and blossom into praying hands.

And then the doctor said, "As citizens of Christian Urakami let us declare our priorities by building the church first. A wooden one will do, until we can rebuild the cathedral again." The crowd was silent.

Almost as soon as the services were over, the hands of the Christians again were busy. They had agreed that the first public building to be raised in the ruins would be the church!

Those who decided to continue living in Nagasaki's Urakami district fashioned small huts for themselves and their families. Dr. Nagai was delighted when his children and their obaason could finally join him again. Dr. Nagai called his hut, *Nyoko-do* or As Yourself Hall, after the famous words of Jesus Christ "Love your neighbor as yourself."

Michael roamed from one hut to another. He was now certain that he would never return to his home. After all, the *chawan* was surely gone, smashed beyond repair in the blast. He gave up hope. One evening Dr. Nagai invited him over to share a humble meal with his family.

Michael looked down at his clothing. He was still wearing the kimono that Thomas had given him back in the sixteenth century. It had not only grown threadbare through the years, but the blackened ruins Michael had been living in made it all the worse for wear. He went to the river to wash himself and his clothing, but the stains were impossible to get out. Still, he felt cleaner.

He wished he had something to give to the Nagai family, some contribution to the meal. They had been so kind to him. But he also knew that Dr. Nagai expected nothing in return. Michael had nearly reached the little *Nyoko-do* hut when someone called, "Michael, wait!"

It was the woman with the sweet potatoes. He stopped and waited for her. As she approached Michael said, "How do you know my name?"

"Didn't you tell me your name?" she asked.

"No, I did not."

"Then someone else told me."

"Oh no you don't," he said. "You're not getting out of it that easy. How do you know me? Did you know Kiyoshi?"

Michael had struck a chord. At the mention of Kiyoshi, her face clouded over. As quickly, she smiled, "Yes, Kiyoshi was a dear family friend."

"Okay, you know Kiyoshi. That's great, but it wasn't the question I meant to ask. I mean, Kiyoshi never introduced us, so he couldn't have told you who I was."

"It is not so important is it?" she asked.

"Yes. It is important to me," Michael told her. There was so little he knew about this world, he at least wanted to know how anyone from this time could know him, without having been introduced.

"All right then," she answered. "So Kiyoshi didn't introduce us. But he spoke to me of the young man who had come to visit him. He told me the young man had knowledge of the *chawan*." Michael was frustrated. It wasn't that he thought she was lying. As a matter of fact, he was certain she was telling the truth. What troubled him was that he was also certain she was hiding something.

"And how did you know the young man was me?" Michael asked.

"You don't exactly blend in. I have watched you. You do not belong here."

"You can tell that, even though everyone around us has been devastated by chaos?" Trying to learn the truth with these questions was like digging for a splinter with no fingernails.

"This," she said, holding up the basket she had carried the other day, "is for you."

"Sweet potatoes?" Michael couldn't believe it. She was trying to placate him with food.

"You want to take something to Dr. Nagai and his family for the meal they are having tonight?" she asked, shoving the basket at him.

Michael took the basket from her and said, "Yes, but how did you know that?"

She looked at him without speaking. Then she touched him again as she had the other day, smoothing his hair from his forehead. "The basket is yours to keep," she said. When she looked away it was as if something was being torn from him besides her gaze. Then she walked away.

"Don't go," he called.

Then he heard Dr. Nagai, "Michael I am glad you could come." Michael debated going after her, but in the end went with Dr. Nagai.

"Here are some sweet potatoes," he said.

The doctor showed him inside the little hut. He handed the basket to the *Obaason*. She bowed and thanked him, "*Arigato!*" She removed several of the sweet potatoes and then handed the basket back to Michael.

Michael tried to tell her to keep it, but she shook her head no. "I cannot accept something so valuable."

Michael was confused and took the ratty old basket. Something lay in the bottom of it. He reached in and pulled out the amber *chawan*. It felt cool in his hands. He felt like kissing the little white crosses decorating the rim. Michael's legs began to tingle. He looked at Dr. Nagai, Makoto, Kayano and their grandmother. They were about the business of life. Tiny Kayano had been so excited to help prepare a meal for her daddy. And though Michael fought it his eyes closed on the little family.

CHAPTER ELEVEN

There were loud explosions. Gunfire sounded in the distance. Michael kept his eyes closed. By wishing the sounds were coming from the television, where his dad could be watching an old war movie, perhaps it would be true. But Michael knew better. The gunfire was not only in the distance it, was all around him. The explosions were too loud to be inside the television set.

He opened his eyes. He saw a vast mountain range dense with pine and beech forests. It was cold and Michael shivered. He was aware of someone beside him. He turned and saw a young man crouched on the ground next to him. He was holding a rifle and his finger was ready on the trigger. He was pointing it at Michael.

"Don't shoot," Michael begged. "Please!"

The soldier studied Michael's face. His body relaxed a bit. He lowered the rifle and said, "What the heck is going on? You sure have a knack for showing up at the most terrible times in my life." The soldier was Daniel.

"Where am I?" Michael asked.

"Still wandering around in time, I see," Daniel said with a wry smile.

"Believe it or not, I've wandered a lot since last I saw you."

To Michael's surprise, Daniel said, "Oh, I believe it."

"You do?"

"Look at you," said Daniel.

Michael was still wearing the tattered kimono he'd worn since the sixteenth century. "The way you keep popping into my life at the worst possible times. You're too young for the army - and that ridiculous outfit…" Daniel said in a sober voice. Then he shook his head. "It's been over two years and you still look like a snot-nosed brat. I don't understand it, but there's no other explanation."

Michael ignored the insult and asked, "Where are we?"

"We're in France," Daniel told him. "It's October, 1944. I'm a soldier in the 442nd Regimental Combat Team, an all Japanese-American Unit. We're Nisei soldiers from Hawaii and also from the mainland, like me."

"You mean America made you fight, after putting your families into internment camps?"

"Actually, we volunteered," Daniel said. "Most of us felt like it was the only way to prove our loyalty to America, the only way to win back honor for our families."

A great burst of light soared in the sky, exploding in the giant fir trees above them. Two bodies slammed into the trench beside them. "Move over, Danny boy," one of them said. The tree burst with the explosion of the artillery and sizzling fragments fell from the sky. Michael was grateful that the foxhole had been dug beneath a huge rock. This rock cover prevented the hot metal and splinters from raining on the men. The makeshift shelter quickly filled with Nisei soldiers.

"You guys okay?" Daniel asked, making sure they hadn't been hit. Daniel took charge easily and Michael could see the men liked him.

"Yes," the men answered. "But we've got to break through to that lost battalion." They discussed their battle plan, paying little attention to Michael. They didn't say anything about how he was dressed. Michael supposed that when you are being shot at continuously, you probably don't pay much attention to what people are wearing. But his teeth chattered and he was sure that he was freezing to death. Daniel took off his wool army jacket and handed it to Michael.

"Here, put this on."

"I don't want to take your coat," Michael protested.

"Don't argue with me, kid. You certainly aren't dressed for the Vosges Mountain cold. Put it on." Michael did so as Daniel explained their mission, "The 1st Battalion, 141st Regiment, 36th Division is trapped. It's a Texas unit and they've advanced too far into the German lines. They're surrounded, with no food or water, and only one radio to make contact. Those that aren't killed by the Germans will soon die of starvation."

"But how can you guys get in there?" Michael wanted to know. "I mean if they're surrounded by the enemy, then, you're marching right into the enemy yourselves."

"That's our orders, little buddy," Daniel told him. "Like I said before, you picked a bad time to drop in." The dozen or so members of Daniel's unit suddenly took stock of Michael.

"Who are you?" they wanted to know. "I don't recognize you from our battalion."

Daniel realized his mistake and sought to repair it, "Leave him be, guys. He's my guardian angel."

"Why weren't we all issued one?" laughed one of the men.

"Oh you got one, Frank," Daniel told him. "You just can't see him. Mine likes to make himself visible once in awhile."

"If he's looking out for you, Daniel, then I guess he can travel with the rest of us," said a skinny soldier wearing glasses.

The one right next to him laughed, adding, "Yeah, maybe he can see to it that our angels are looking out for us too. Our unit could use some heavenly protection."

One of the men said, "That's the only direction people like us can look to for help. Japanese-Americans are a pretty cheap commodity here on earth."

"Enough chit chat. Are we ready?" Daniel asked them.

"Let's go for broke," they answered.

Daniel looked at Michael and said, "That's our motto,

'Go For Broke'. It means, shoot the works. We're giving everything we got." Michael nodded and stood to go with them.

"No," Daniel put up his hand. "You stay here."

"Alone? I don't think so. I'm going with you and you can't stop me." But Michael wasn't quick enough to ward off Daniel's fist. It hit him square in the jaw. Michael felt a different kind of cold as unconsciousness covered him.

When he awoke a short time later he was alone. He crawled from the trench in search of Daniel and his buddies. The terrain had been flooded by the Germans and was thick with mud. Michael kept going though. It was better than waiting alone. He saw several explosions of tree bursts. He crawled what seemed like hours up the craggy, dense hill of the Vosges Forest. The hill was steep and there were numerous deep gullies cut in the side. The entire ridge was thick with trees and undergrowth.

He was grateful for the night and hoped enemy snipers wouldn't spot him. Then a barrage of shells came crashing down and he heard Daniel's voice, "Take cover."

Michael saw him and the others roll into a trench and he crawled through the mud and fell in beside them.

"I told you to stay put," Daniel said.

"And I refused," Michael replied. Daniel didn't say any more. They stayed in the trench only a short while and then trudged onward.

Michael followed them as they continued their advance through enemy lines. The mountain air was freezing. Daniel's coat helped but Michael was still wearing the sandals Thomas had given him. The pain in his feet was terrible and they felt oddly like someone else's had been attached improperly to his legs.

The forest was so dense with growth and the fog so heavy that Michael hardly knew night had fallen until Daniel said, "Let's rest for a moment." A previously used foxhole provided them shelter and they inched close to one another for added warmth. It was pitch black.

Someone crawled next to him. It was Daniel. He handed him a pair of boots and trousers. Michael took them and said, "Thanks." He didn't ask where Daniel had found them. One of the men lit a cigarette, illuminating the bloodstains on the trousers and the mud, still wet, clinging to the side of the boots. Michael tried not to think about the body that had worn the articles previously.

"It was a German," Daniel said, as if he knew what Michael had been thinking.

"Thank you," Michael said again to let Daniel know that it didn't matter. He was so cold he would have put the boots on even if they had been from one of the Nisei. All the same, he was glad it had been a German.

German artillery continued to pound them on all sides. Michael wondered if they would make it. He had no knowledge of this particular battle. As for Daniel, he only knew that his uncle, like his mother, had died. But he didn't know how or where. As a matter of fact, his grandmother had never even told him that her brother had served in the war. Why, he wondered? So much of the Japanese-American experience was buried, never discussed.

The Germans had the advantage from above them. They could watch their every move. They'd already shot down many of the Nisei as they made their way towards the lost battalion. And though they were annihilated as they marched, their orders from

General John E. Dahlquist were to continue on that path.

They'd made their way through mountains, mud, and mine fields with a spirit that Michael had come to know well. They tried to keep their minds occupied with positive images and Michael listened as they discussed their hopes and plans for the future.

"Boy, I'd give anything to be sitting at that white and red checkered table at the local soda fountain," said one of the men.

"Yeah, we had one of those in my home town. I can see that sweet little waitress now, serving up the thickest chocolate milk shakes you ever tasted," said another.

"C'mon you guys, you're making my belly growl," laughed Daniel. "I can smell a big juicy hamburger on the grill." Michael was sitting next to Daniel and he reminded him, "Don't forget the hot French fries."

"French fries make me think of Martie," Daniel told him. "I met her in the camp the year before I enlisted. We had a great time together. She sure loved French fries!"

"Was she your girlfriend?" Michael asked him.

"We never got around to calling it that," Daniel said. "In the camps, life wasn't really so simple. I loved her; I told myself that many times. I guess we skipped all the usual dating rituals when I enlisted. We went from dating to talking about getting married and having a family. I don't remember if I ever told her that I loved her. When I enlisted, she cried. Yet she never once tried to talk me out of it."

Daniel dug deep in his backpack and shared his rations with Michael. When Daniel gave the order to move out, he actually waited for Michael to come with him.

A soldier came running up to Daniel and said, "General Dahlquist has just phoned headquarters and told them to keep us going. 'Don't let them stop,' is what he told the officers. He doesn't care what happens to us does he," the soldier said rather than asked. "It doesn't matter that we're being gunned down like tin ducks in a carnival shooting gallery."

Daniel put his arm around the soldier. "We're the best they've got right now. Don't forget the promise we made to our parents when we left the camp." The soldier stood a bit straighter after that. As the unit continued on, the soldier dropped back.

Michael took the opportunity to ask Daniel, "What promise did you guys make to your parents?"

Daniel answered, "That we would defend our country to the best of our ability, that we would not bring shame upon our family, and that we would act with honor always.

"Our families' tomorrows may be measured by what our Nisei battalions prove today. We know that we're loyal Americans. The difference between us and other Americans is that we have to prove it. That's just the way it is." Michael couldn't see Daniel's face but he could hear the pride in his voice. "I'm getting a job as soon as this war is over. I don't care what it is. I want our life back." Michael said nothing. He sensed Daniel needed to talk.

"You know, my Dad died shortly after he was returned to us in the camp. I know that he died with a broken heart. I was so angry then. I would blow up at Mom when she tried to take up for America. But deep inside, I knew she was right. It wasn't America that had treated us unjustly. It was some people in America. There is a difference you know."

Then they encountered heavier machine gun fire from the hill on their right. Daniel tried to pinpoint the gunner's nest. He shoved Michael back and hissed, "Take cover," as he maneuvered under fire toward the crest of the hill. As before, Michael couldn't obey. He was right behind him. As they advanced, men were falling all around them. The soldier Daniel had spoken to about promises fell. Daniel turned and ordered the rest of the men to "Take cover!" Then he continued to crawl to the wounded soldier and dragged him from the line of fire. Before he could reach the brush he was heading for, the gunners blasted Daniel's body. He fell with a sickening thud.

Michael ran, caught up to him and pulled him as gently as he could off the top of the other soldier. He got him into the shelter of some thick brush. Then he crawled back and dragged the other soldier next to Daniel. "How's George?" Daniel whispered in pain.

Michael shook his head. The other soldier was dead. "Eternal rest grant…" Daniel choked the words, "unto him dear Lord."

Michael saw then that Daniel had been shot more than once. There were six bullet wounds and blood was rushing from each of them. His eyes searched Michael's face. Michael didn't say anything. He didn't have to. Daniel knew.

He reached with a trembling hand and made the sign of the cross. "Oh my God, I am heartily sorry for having offended Thee…" he began to choke again and Michael lifted his head and cradled it in his arms. "Help me… Please," Daniel said to him. Michael remembered the act of contrition from catechism class. He tried to steady his voice as he recited for Daniel, "And I detest all my sins because I dread the loss of Heaven and the pains of Hell; but most of all because they have offended Thee, my God, Who art all good and deserving of all my love," Michael stifled a sob.

Daniel struggled to finish, "I firmly resolve with the help of Thy Grace, to confess my sins, to do penance, and to amend my life."

Michael finished with, "Amen."

Michael held Daniel in his arms and could actually feel his life ebb from his body. "You made me laugh," Daniel told him.

"Don't try to talk," As painful as it was for Daniel to say them, his words were breaking Michael's heart.

Daniel's voice continued to weaken. "No, listen, you've got to promise me…"

"Anything," Michael said, just wanting Daniel to rest.

"Tell Mom that I died with honor. Tell her that I died thanking her for raising me to be honorable." Michael was crying openly now. But Daniel had no time. He fought to say all the words in his heart.

"I am her only son. She will be heartbroken." Michael nodded, and remembered that he had failed to take the message to Thomas' mother. How would he get a message to Daniel's mother? He didn't know if he would ever be in her time again. She died too, before he was born.

Michael looked straight into Daniel's eyes and said, "I'll tell her, Daniel. Don't worry. Somehow, I will get word to her."

Daniel's head moved slightly. "Thanks, buddy. I'm glad you were here." His breathing was ragged. He coughed again and his entire body seemed to contract with pain. He looked at Michael and said, "I don't feel so alone. You're like family somehow." He shuddered violently. A gurgle from low in his throat erupted. And then he was still.

Michael brought the dark haired head of his uncle to his chest. He buried his own head in Daniel's chest and he wept. He wept that Daniel would not have the chance to marry Martie, the girl waiting for him behind that barbed wire back home. And he wept for his grandmother, who would soon learn that her brother had been killed so far from home.

Michael had known him as a friend. He had crossed the ocean and left his family to come here and fight, to prove his loyalty to a country that had turned his family into prisoners. But like the others in his lineage, Daniel had been filled with an honor and a raw courage that saw duty to its end.

Michael saw Daniel's Tommy gun lying by his side. He laid his head back on the cold ground. He picked up Daniel's Tommy gun and ran. He ran like the others, with their Bonsai charge. He ran up what they had called, 'Suicide Hill,' blasting the Tommy gun all the while. Blindly he pulled the trigger at the German machine gun nests, taking out anyone in his path. His heart beat with anger. Anger at all he had witnessed since he began this terrible journey through time. He pulled the trigger and fired at the injustice of martyrdom suffered by Thomas and his friends. He pulled the trigger and tried to blow away the horror of Nagasaki after the bomb. He pulled the trigger to obliterate the pain of Midori's death. He shot Daniel's Tommy gun at the Germans to wipe away the man who had killed him. And then he stopped. He stood and surveyed the bodies around him. Germans, some with eyes still wide open stared at him from the side of death. One of them moaned. Michael was torn between what he had done and the anger and grief of Daniel's death. He turned away. The faint cry of the man, who was breathing his last, called to him. Michael went over to the man. He looked at his blood soaked chest. Life was fading away quickly.

This man looks like my father, he thought. And I have killed him. Michael knew then what it must have been like for his own ancestors as they entered the war, perhaps to fight against men who looked like their fathers or brothers.

He heard again the tree bursts overhead. Too late, he ran for cover. He felt something slice through his body with a terrible heat. He fell to the ground. Just before he slipped into unconsciousness he wondered how he could be hurt in this time, and yet walked through the atomic bomb untouched.

He was dimly aware of someone lifting him and carrying him. He could hear the sounds of their boots crunching the frozen layer of mud. But he could not open his eyes.

He slept. But there were times in his sleep when he heard voices. The voices spoke to him. "You're going to be okay," a man's voice said.

Another voice was that of a woman. He felt her stroke his hair, and then he dreamed of the mysterious woman from Nagasaki that had done the same.

There were other voices too, but he couldn't always make out what they were saying. His body felt as if it were rocking at times, like he was drifting out to sea. There were times when he tried to open his eyes, but could not. He was in a deep sleep and yet it was strange that you could know this while in such a state.

Finally, after being disconnected from his body, from life, he opened his eyes. A brightness so intense it hurt assaulted him and he closed his eyes quickly against the glare. "It is okay," he heard a man say. "Open your eyes slowly. It will take a few moments for them to adjust." Michael did as he was told and found it to be true.

As his eyes were adjusting they were also taking in his surroundings. He was on a small cot in a room that was lined with metal objects. Metal filing cabinets, a metal desk and even the walls looked metal. Michael saw a window; no it was more like a porthole. It was a porthole. He was on a ship.

The man was wearing the white uniform of a navy officer. "I am Dr. Joseph. You have slept for a long while. But you have awakened just in time." He lifted Michael into a sitting position. "Come," he said, "We are in New York Harbor. See the Statue of Liberty?"

Michael walked with his assistance to the window and looked out at America. His heart swelled at the sight. He turned to the doctor and said, "My friend, Daniel… He was killed,"

"I know," answered the doctor. A silence followed.

Then Michael asked, "How long have I been here?"

"You were carried by one of your Nisei comrades from the Vosges Mountain battlefield to a medic station. You weren't wearing any dog tags. The man who carried you either didn't know your name, or chose not to give it. He said only that you were Daniel's angel.

From there you were sent to the hospital in France, where we cared for you until we were transferred home. We have known you only as 'Daniel's angel' but we knew that you had to be American. Why else would you have been on suicide hill?"

Michael remembered it all. He asked, "Did the 442nd save the 'Lost Battalion'?"

"You bet they did," the doctor said. "They tromped up that hill, and by the time that they had rescued those 211 Texans, they had suffered 800 casualties."

Someone knocked on the door and the doctor went to answer it. When he came back he handed Michael a pile of clothes.

"I think this will fit better than what we found you in. It's time for you to get dressed. Then after we fill out a few papers, we can see about getting you home."

Michael took the clothes without saying anything. He couldn't go back home if it was still the 1940s. The only hope he had was that small amber *chawan* and he hadn't seen it since he'd sat in Dr. Nagai's little hut in Nagasaki.

The doctor was nearly out the door when he stopped and came back. "By the way, I thought you might be interested to know, those buddies of yours are going to be recognized for their valor. Your families were treated shamefully by this nation. But your battalion carried honor and loyalty right into the battles that cost many of them their lives.

"The soldier who carried you down told us that you were with I Company. Your company started into that battle with 200 men. Ten survived. Every time one of their names was put in for the Medal of Honor, it was downgraded to a Distinguished Service Cross. Only one was granted. Despite all that, I'm sure they will go on to become the most decorated unit of their size in Army history.

"Their courage will not be forgotten." The doctor turned on his heel and went out the door. Michael walked over to the mirror on the door and studied his reflection. Had he aged? He didn't feel like a 14 year old.

A gentle knock sounded at the door and a woman's voice called, "Are you ready to go topside?" her voice had a familiar quality to it. Michael still in his underwear, grabbed the blanket off the bed, wrapped it around him and opened the door. A nurse stood waiting for him.

It was the woman he'd met in Nagasaki. "I know you," he said, "Who are you?"

"Think of me as your guardian, sent from heaven to help you."

"Why can't you tell me the truth?"

"Surely you have learned that truth is the first casualty of war," she said to him. Michael bit back his anger. After all, he'd not been truthful with those he'd met. Daniel was the only one he'd told the whole truth. And Daniel had called him his guardian angel.

Michael had a sudden impression of Daniel in the woman's face. Following his hunch, he asked her, "Did you know Daniel Endo?"

"No," she said. "I never had the pleasure of knowing him. But I've heard he was a wonderful man." Michael believed she was telling the truth. So his hunch was wrong. She wasn't his grandmother at a younger time.

She walked over to a set of lockers behind the door of his room. Opening the middle one, she reached in and pulled out a bundle. She turned and handed it to Michael. "I believe this belongs to you."

Holding the blanket around his neck with one hand, he took the bundle with his other, staring as the layers of cloth fell away from the object. It was the amber *chawan* with the tiny white crosses.

He looked at the woman and begged, "Who are you? Please, tell me your name." She took the cloth from his hands and he felt the coolness of the ancient amber pottery. His legs began to tingle. Michael didn't want to leave her. Though he could be going home, he struggled against it. He wanted to know who she was. She hadn't even given him her name.

But the prickling continued in his legs and though he struggled to keep her in sight, she began to fade. Just as his eyes closed, he glimpsed the silver medal around her neck. It was a miraculous medal. Instinctively, he grabbed for the one around his neck, the one Fr. Kolbe had given him. It was gone.

CHAPTER TWELVE

Michael held his breath and forced his eyes open. The woman's fading image strengthened. It was like watching an outline in a coloring book as a crayon covers it, back and forth. Michael didn't stop to wonder how wise it was to have stalled his travel this time.

The medal around the woman's neck, the familiarity he felt towards her, his yearning to know who she was and what she meant to him, all these things seemed more urgent.

And he felt confident since he'd managed to control something for once. She stood there just as before, the cloth still in her hands.

"No," she said to him, "You must not stay. It is time for you to return home."

"I knew it," Michael said, his heart pounding. "You are traveling through time also. You were in Nagasaki. You know how to direct where you are going in the past don't you?"

Instead of answering him she insisted, "You must go. We do not have much time. Now that you are awake, they will begin to question you. How can you explain who you are? Can you tell them how you managed to end up in the mountains of France with Daniel and his battalion?"

Michael figured if she wasn't going to answer questions, neither would he. He couldn't really answer hers anyway. But she could answer his. "Where did you get that medal? I had one like it. Where is it? What have they done with it?"

"Perhaps it was lost between the battle and your transfer. You shall have another, I promise."

"No! Medals like mine are not easy to come by. A saint gave mine to me. Can you duplicate that?"

"Do you want to return home, or do you want to search for the medal? Surely you realize the trouble you are in if you stay."

"Apparently you know all about the troubles of time travel. If you aren't in deep trouble being here, then why am I?"

"Unlike you, I have a perfectly good reason to be here. I am seen simply as a nurse. We are often ignored until needed. You, on the other hand, were taken from a battlefield by a fellow soldier who would not, or could not tell us who you were. You were wearing no dog tags, had no identification, and you were unconscious with no visible wounds or reason for such a condition."

Michael remembered the searing heat that had sliced through his body as he fell on the battlefield. "No wounds? But I felt a terrible pain."

"What you felt was Daniel's pain."

"That can't be. I was hurt… cut, when I squeezed the broken bits of the *chawan* in the sixteenth century."

"You were the cause of those injuries, not the past. You cannot be hurt in a time in which you do not exist. The past is a different dimension from your world. You must have sustained some kind of injury to your body in your own time in order for an actual abrasion to appear in the past."

"You mean I am still back there? I am still in my own time, while I am here in the past?"

"Your body is there, yes. But you are not conscious. Your awareness can only be in one place at a time." This was too much for Michael to try and comprehend. His body could be in two places, his mind only in one?

She tried to explain, "It is your mind that has brought your image to this place. Think of the past

128

and present as one bolt of material. The present spins the strands of life into cloth. That cloth contains fibers of the past within the fabric. When one travels to the past, they analyze the threads. They discover history by following the fibers that led to certain events."

As she had done in Nagasaki, the woman reached up and stroked his forehead. Her gesture stirred deep and tender feelings in Michael. It was as if this small action had knit their hearts together. "By studying past events, your awareness is in the fibers of the past, though your body remains in that present time, waiting for you to return to create a pattern of your own."

"You are a relative of mine aren't you?" Michael asked her.

"That will be answered in your own time." She shook her head and said, "There are more important things to be concerned with at the moment.

"You must be careful. What do you think the government will do with a boy that appears from nowhere? You have no records in this time, no way to prove who you are. You cannot just walk past these officers without following certain procedures. There are questions they will ask, papers they will want to fill out. Mountains of red tape…"

"Tell me who you are and I will do as you say," Michael told her.

She studied his face. Michael felt ashamed as he stared back into her eyes. He didn't mean to be obstinate. But he had to know for sure.

"I promise that when you return to your time, you will have your answer. That is the most I can tell you about me. You and I have been granted a great gift in our travels. We must not become so greedy for answers that we ask the wrong questions."

What were the right questions, Michael wondered. He had asked many since his journey began, but they usually revolved around him. Like where am I? Who are you? What is the date?

She took the *chawan* from him and said, "The past speaks to the present. It would be wise to

listen. But remember, the cloth you are studying connects to your own life. You must be very careful not to unravel the strands. By tugging too hard at a certain thread in the cloth, you could unravel the fabric of life that destiny has planned for you."
Somehow her explanation made a bizarre kind of sense.

"Okay, so I won't pester you anymore about who you are. But can you at least tell me how you came to be here? What brought you to the past? Are you connected to the *chawan* too?"

For a long second she seemed about to answer him. In the end she did not. She reached for the medal around her neck and fingered it. "Michael, you told me that a saint had given you a medal like this one."

"He was a saint!"

"The medal is a sacramental," she said, ignoring Michael's assertion. "While sacraments actually deliver grace to our souls, the sacramental reminds us of our faith; it teaches us, as well as those around us, it prepares us to receive that grace. The same saint gave this medal to me. Now I want you to have it."

Michael's heart was pounding in his chest. It seemed to be sending a message to his brain. But he couldn't read it. "No, I can't take yours," he told her.

"Michael, please remember that though the world is filled with evil, saints still surround us. If we follow them in faith, we too can weave a pattern that is worth preserving for future generations." Then she thrust the *chawan* back at him.

Michael took it. Immediately he felt the tingling in his legs. Just as she started to fade she thrust the medal towards him, "Take this. Now!" He nearly reached out and grasped it before his eyelashes fell. The faintest touch of the medal lingered on his fingers and then faded with her. Her voice, the words she spoke were the last things to fade. He heard her say, "I love you, Michael! I will always love you."

And then he was lying on his back. Michael could tell he was on a mattress and not a futon. He heard the springs squeak as he moved. A motor softly hummed in the distance. Over the gentle hum he heard voices. They were familiar voices.

He opened his eyes bit by bit. He glimpsed first the pattern of the cloth that covered him. It was a quilt. The log cabin quilt his mother had finished for him just before she died. His eyes shot wide open and there sat his father and grandmother, each in chairs beside his bed.

"Thank God," cried his father, who stood and gathered Michael in his arms. Michael tried to remember the last time his father had held him but could not.

"I was so afraid I was losing you too," he said after finally releasing him.

"How long have I been like this?" Michael asked.

His grandmother squeezed his hand, "Almost a week. You gave us quite a scare. You simply went to sleep as we were having tea. You wouldn't wake up and the doctors had no idea what was wrong."

"It wasn't the tea, because your grandmother drank it and she was fine," his father told him.

"Grandmother, didn't you tell Dad it was the *chawan*?"

His father said, "What about the *chawan*?"

"What are you talking about Michael?" His grandmother looked at him in bewilderment. Did she really have no idea? How could she not know?

She shrugged, "I told him you sipped your tea from the *chawan*. More than that - I don't know. After you went to sleep I regretted having given you the tea set. I really wished I'd given you the swords." She looked at Michael and said, "But I promised your mother before she died…"

"My mother?" Michael's heart closed in on itself. A great pain crushed his chest and he heard again the words, "…I love you, Michael."

He was stunned as he realized what he had lost. So much he could have asked her. So much he wanted to tell her. "She was my mother..." Michael said aloud.

He thought of all he had witnessed since his journey began. He remembered what she had said about tugging too hard for certain threads. She had told him, "Saints still surround us..." and he felt her presence as never before. Michael saw the worried looks exchanged between his father and grandmother. He tried to explain, "I've seen so many awful things."

His grandmother held onto his hand. "You were having terrible nightmares. You pulled the IV from your wrist and scratched your hands with the needle." Michael pulled his hand away and looked. There were faint marks on the palms where the scratches had healed.

His father placed his hand on Michael's head and said, "Thank God, you're okay now, son."

His grandmother leaned over and kissed him, brushing the hair off his brow just the way his mother had done. "You woke up just in time for your birthday, Michael. Tomorrow, you'll be fifteen," she said. "I'm going to leave you two alone now. I better start dinner or we'll be sending out again, Richard." His father sat in the chair beside him and they were silent, each thinking their own thoughts.

Later that evening, Michael awoke to darkness. He rose from his bed and made his way down the familiar stairs. A light was on in the family room and Michael went in.

He found his grandmother packaging up the *chawan*, returning the utensils to the *chabako*. She looked up as he entered the room.

"You would have thought I would have done this weeks ago, but I have been so preoccupied." Michael thought her hand trembled just a bit.

"Grandmother, I just remembered, what about your teaching position? You didn't give it up did you?"

"No dear. I tried. The director has granted me a leave of absence. Funny to be granted a leave when

132

you haven't even made a showing." Michael smiled at her little joke.

"I'm sorry to have worried you and Dad."

"I'm just glad that you are well again. I kept going over in my mind that afternoon. How you lifted the *chawan* to your lips, sipped the tea and then, as if you were in a trance of some kind, you placed the *chawan* back on the table and as you were closing your eyes you simply lay back against the couch. We sent the remains of your tea to be tested and the results showed only tea. I wished that it were only a ploy of yours to get me to stay. But the doctors said your reflexes were that of a comatose patient."

"I wouldn't have gone that far to keep you here, Grandmother," Michael said, hurt that she would think he could be that devious.

"I knew that, Michael. But still I hoped. You see I preferred that to the unknown illness that had stolen you from us. It reminded me so much of when your mother was dying. But then we knew that she was ill. With you, it was so unexpected and there was no illness to blame." Michael wanted to explain. But if she didn't know already...

"I often thought of your mother as I sat by your bedside. You know, you mentioned the *chawan* earlier. It made me remember something else.

"As your mother was dying she had a couple of peculiar requests. I didn't think much of it then; she was so ill. I simply promised her that I would do as she asked."

"And what did she ask?" Michael whispered. He didn't know why he was whispering. It was as though a great secret was about to be told, and even though no one else was around to hear, he whispered the importance of it because speaking of it loudly would shatter its significance.

"She made me promise that I would give this to you," she pointed at the *chabako*. "And I was to give it to you before you reached manhood." Michael's face flushed in embarrassment.

His grandmother laughed and said, "I think you are quite a young man, Michael. And that day in the garden I realized, as we spoke about your relationship with your father, that I had almost waited too long. You were showing definite signs of your own personality.

"After I gave it to you I noticed your disappointment. Then when you invited me over and performed the Tea Ceremony, I was sure I had waited too long. You were definitely a man. And a gentleman at that." She winked at him.

"But when you went into that deep unconscious sleep, I forgot about the *chawan*, I forgot Laurie's insistence that I give it to you. I didn't remember until you spoke of the *chawan* when you awoke.

"Laurie had a fascination for it in those days before she died. She would ask me to hand it to her at times when I knew she was suffering from a severe bout of pain. I asked her once what holding the *chawan* did for her."

"What did she tell you, Grandmother?" Michael wanted to know.

"It didn't make any sense to me, Michael," she said, shutting the door on the *chabako*.

"I don't care if it made sense or not. I just want to know what she said."

"Yes, I suppose you do," she agreed. "You lost her when you were so young. She must have been thinking that. And she had spent so much time trying to finish the sewing on the quilt she was making for you. Those two ideas must have gotten twisted in her mind. Because she said, 'I am weaving a fabric of my life for Michael.'

"I asked her what she was trying to say. I mean you can't weave with a teacup! She was so sick by that time. She just smiled at me and said, 'Mother, I am placing a pattern of my healthy self in the cloth of his life.'"

Michael felt the presence of his mother, the woman who had followed him through the tea, or rather he had followed her.

"She made me promise that I would not only give you the *chabako*, I had to be certain you knew how to use it. In my grief at losing her, and then my joy in watching you grow, I nearly forgot. That day in the garden I remembered. It was as if she stood beside me, whispering the promise I had made to her so long ago."

He remembered Daniel's dying words. He tried not to think of the fact that he was unable to keep that promise to him. At least his grandmother had been able to keep her promise to his mother. Just then he remembered something.

"Grandmother, you said that my mother had a couple requests. What was the other one?"

His grandmother picked up the *chabako* and carried it to the hallway, placing it near the front door. When she came back into the room she said, "I thought you'd never ask. "Hand me my purse," she told him. Michael reached for the black leather bag and passed it to his grandmother.

"Laurie was very insistent that I pass this item on to you. But only, she said, after I was certain you were familiar with the *Chado*. She said that it wouldn't make sense to you until you understood the Way of Tea." Opening the bag, his grandmother reached in and pulled out an envelope. She studied it for a moment, almost caressing it before passing it to Michael.

"These are very like a person's last words. She told me to tell you that. Only after saying that could I hand you this," and she handed it to Michael.

"It was the last bit of writing she ever did. She'd written one to me the day before." His grandmother laughed again.

"My girl was wise. Had she not done so, I would have been sorely tempted in these last ten years to read yours."

Michael took the envelope and held it tight. His grandmother said, "I'll leave you alone for a moment. I think I will fetch us a glass of lemonade."

As she walked out Michael opened the envelope carefully. He read what his mother had written.

Dear Michael,

So much I will miss of your life and yet how much more I was given than I ever expected. I am glad that you were strong enough to engage in the Tea Ceremony. Had you not had the courage to humble yourself in such a way, I would not have been given the brief moments that I cherished.

As I wasted away before your young eyes, I was able to find peace and strength in studying the pattern of our past. And I was able to witness before I left, the fine man you would become. I was able to attend to you on the ship as we returned from France. You spoke to me in your sleep. You told me things about my Uncle Daniel that I never knew. I came to know him through your words. You wrestled in your dreams with the promise you made to tell his mother, my grandmother, of his last words. I wrote them down as I sat beside you. Just before I came back to this sick bed of mine, I made sure the letter was posted to her.

So you were able to fulfill that promise, Michael. Daniel's mother knew he died with honor and thoughts of her. I can finally give you my Miraculous Medal. Fr. Kolbe gave it to me also. I was so happy to learn on the ship that the medal was important to you - that sainthood was something you honored. Remember Michael that saints surround you. All you have to do is follow the threads of their lives. And don't forget:

I love you, Michael! I will always love you. God bless and keep you, my son. And may we one day be united in heaven in that blessed communion of saints.
All my Love, Mother.

He folded the letter and placed it neatly in the envelope. There in the bottom was the Miraculous Medal that hung around his mother's neck. He pulled it out, crossed himself with it, kissed it and placed it around his own neck. "Oh Mary, conceived without sin, pray for us who have recourse to thee," he whispered.

His grandmother came back into the room and handed him a glass of lemonade, "Now that my promise to her has been kept, I'm going to give you something you've wanted all along." She picked up the narrow wooden box that contained the samurai swords. She brought it to the coffee table and placed it in front of Michael.

He didn't move to open them. He sat there, remembering. His grandmother opened the box for him. She removed the *katana*. Michael stared at the glistening blade and took it as she offered it to him. This blade had severed the ears of his friends. It had been the last one Kosuma Takeya had made before turning towards Christ and a life of peace. Reflected in the blade Michael saw the martyrs, as they were ready to die for their faith. He saw the tears of the Nagasaki Christians, and Midori Nagai's spirit as it rose from the ash to embrace her grieving husband. He saw the boy he used to be as he stood in his *kata* stance, pretending to be a samurai aimed to kill.

Michael got up and went into the hallway. He picked up the *chabako* and brought it into the room and placed it on the table near the swords. "I know now that the strength of a man is not found in the weapons he makes for war."

Michael thought of the 800 casualties of the 442nd as they charged up Suicide Hill. Closing the lid on the swords, he said, "I understand that it's not in being ready to kill that a man shows his strength, but in being ready to die for peace. Grandmother, if you don't mind, I would like to keep this." He picked up the *chabako* and looked at his grandmother.

"Of course, Michael," she told him. "It's your choice. Go ahead and take it to your room. But hurry back, dinner is nearly ready and I hear your father's car in the drive."

He gave her a quick hug and turned to take the tea set to his room. He thought about what his mother had told him about the past and present. He knew that he would no longer be ashamed of the face he wore. The fabric of his life had been fashioned by the pain and suffering of his ancestors.

He promised himself that he would pick up the strands of their lives and weave them into his own. He would live his life so that his children would find pride in the pattern of his past.

He heard his mother's words reaching out to him, "You have shown me great honor; you have made me certain of your character. I am very proud of you." Like a fine gossamer strand he clasped it and carried it with him.

He placed the *chabako* on his closet shelf. He opened the little door and taking the letter from his mother, he placed it inside with the *chawan*. Her spirit softly brushed past him, like a wisp of angel hair. He brushed his bangs from his forehead as she did each time they'd met. "I love you too, Mom. And I always will."